Vampire Kisses 6

Royal Blood

PRAISE FOR

Vampire Kisses

An ALA Quick Pick for Reluctant Young Adult Readers
A New York Public Library Book for the Teen Age

"All in all, a good read for those who want a vampire love story without the gore."   —*School Library Journal*

"As in her *Teenage Mermaid*, Schreiber adds some refreshing twists to genre archetypes and modern-day stereotypes."
—*Publishers Weekly*

"Horror hooks such as a haunted mansion, a romantic teenage vampire, and a dark heroine who wins against the golden guys make this a title that readers will bite into with Goth gusto."   —*The Bulletin of the Center for Children's Books*

"Schreiber uses a careful balance of humor, irony, pathos, and romance as she develops a plot that introduces the possibility of a real vampire."   —ALA *Booklist*

Kissing Coffins
Vampire Kisses 2

"Raven is exactly the kind of girl a Goth can look up to."
—*Morbid Outlook* magazine

"Readers will love this funny novel with bite!"
—*Wow* magazine

Vampireville
Vampire Kisses 3

"A fun, fast read for vampire fans."—*School Library Journal*

Dance with a Vampire
Vampire Kisses 4

"This novel, like the first three, is never short on laughs and shudders. Alexander is as romantic as ever, and Raven is still delightfully earthy. Schreiber again concocts a lively and suspenseful story that ends on a tantalizing cliffhanger. Fans of the series will be anxious to find out whether Raven's relationship with Alexander will survive." —*VOYA*

"A good choice for Goth lovers and fans of romantic vampire stories."
—*School Library Journal*

Also by Ellen Schreiber

VAMPIRE KISSES

VAMPIRE KISSES 2: KISSING COFFINS

VAMPIRE KISSES 3: VAMPIREVILLE

VAMPIRE KISSES 4: DANCE WITH A VAMPIRE

VAMPIRE KISSES 5: THE COFFIN CLUB

VAMPIRE KISSES: BLOOD RELATIVES

TEENAGE MERMAID

COMEDY GIRL

Ellen Schreiber

Vampire Kisses 6

Royal Blood

KATHERINE TEGEN BOOKS
An Imprint of HarperCollins Publishers

Katherine Tegen Books is an imprint of HarperCollins Publishers.

Vampire Kisses 6: Royal Blood
Copyright © 2009 by Ellen Schreiber
All rights reserved. Printed in the United States of America.

www.harperteen.com
Library of Congress Cataloging-in-Publication Data
Schreiber, Ellen.
Vampire kisses 6 : royal blood / Ellen Schreiber. — 1st ed.
p. cm.
"Katherine Tegen Books."
Summary: While fending off Trevor, her nemesis at school with whom she must work on an important project, sixteen-year-old Raven is distracted by finally meeting her vampire-boyfriend Alexander's parents and trying to foil their plan that could jeopardize her future with him.
ISBN 978-0-06-128887-6
[1. Vampires—Fiction. 2. Family life—Fiction. 3. High schools—Fiction. 4. Schools—Fiction.]
I. Title. II. Title: Vampire kisses six. III. Title: Royal blood.
PZ7.S3787Vamf 2009   2008051774
[Fic]—dc22   CIP
                                                                                                              AC

Typography by Sasha Illingworth
09 10 11 12 13 LP/RRDB 10 9 8 7 6 5 4 3 2 1
❖
First Edition

To my husband, Eddie,
with love and vampire kisses

CONTENTS

"Welcome to the family."

—Mrs. Sterling

T he letter arrived mysteriously.

I imagined the deliverer was an enigmatic figure masked in a centuries-old black hooded cloak, slipping undetected through the darkness past the Mansion's wrought-iron gate. He may have approached the Sterlings' haunted-looking house in a hearse. Or perhaps he'd flown over the menacing fence in the form of a bat.

By nightfall, the Mansion's mailbox was usually as hollow as an empty coffin, sitting lonely at the bottom of Benson Hill, at the end of a long and windy driveway. So the letter would go unnoticed for several hours as I was stolen away in Alexander's attic room, pressed against my vampire boyfriend's deathly pale, but full of life, lips.

Several weeks had passed since Alexander and I had returned from our adventure in Hipsterville, and though Alexander hadn't bitten me, he did make this mortal feel a part of the Underworld. During that time, we began to experience the vampire life without distractions. There was no school to interrupt my daytime sleep, no Trevor Mitchell to be a thorn in my side, and no Dullsville High students to ridicule my dark attire. There were no teen vampires lurking in the cemetery, disrupting Alexander's and my stardust dates. No threat of a preteen Nosferatu attempting to turn my younger brother and his nerd-mate immortal. Free of the feuding Maxwells, Alexander and I were now able to unite our mortal and immortal worlds as one.

I was also beginning to do something I'd never had the opportunity to do before—make the Mansion my home. And why shouldn't I? On a dare, in my youth, I'd snuck into it by squeezing through the abandoned estate's broken basement window. Now, invited, I could confidently walk right up its splintered stone path and through its creaky unlocked front door.

I had never been so happy in my life.

I transformed the Mansion into Alexander's and my private vampire castle. I felt like a medieval queen and Alexander was my handsome king. Instead of spending the rest of summer break in my tiny bedroom, I suddenly had full reign over a palatial estate. I replaced Alexander's torn and aged bedroom curtain with a brand-new black lace one. I added some candelabras I'd found at a rummage sale to the ones his grandmother had brought from Romania. I placed black roses in pewter vases and lavender-scented votives and rose petals on all the empty antique end tables.

Jameson, Alexander's butler, didn't seem to mind. In fact, he even appeared to delight in a woman's (or, in my case, teen girl's) touch around the barren estate.

It even seemed like the Mansion itself was amused by my presence. The floors appeared to give an extra squeak when I ran over them, as if the uneven boards were greeting my stay. The wind sounded louder than I'd remembered as it whistled through the cracked windowpanes. The creaking in the foundation warmly echoed off the hollow walls at a higher volume than it had before.

The massive house glistened with candles and cobwebs.

During the day I nestled in Alexander's corpse-cold arms, cuddling in his coffin. At night we cranked Rob Zombie and had midnight showings of *Fright Night*.

Alexander gave me the next best thing to a sparkling diamond ring—a dresser drawer. His dresser was as ancient as Dracula himself. A family-owned chipped oak bureau with glass knobs held his clothes in five three-foot-long drawers. Alexander emptied the middle one for me, to be filled with anything I liked. One of the glass handles had broken and he replaced it with a wooden raven. There was even a lock on the dresser. At first I thought it was a facade, but on closer inspection it was revealed to be real. Whereas everything in my bedroom—clothes, magazines, hair products—was cast about in an unorganized mess, my drawer at the Mansion was in perfect order. Alexander brought out the best in me. It held a pair of socks, my Emily the Strange hoodie, a few T-shirts, and a bat-shaped sachet. I often felt jealous of the accessories I left there, which got to call the Mansion their home, while I returned to my house on Dullsville Drive.

I even managed to bake at the Mansion. I prepared ghost-shaped cookies, cupcakes with witch hats, and chocolate Rice Krispie treats. With my new independence I found a side of me that I didn't know existed.

My parents were pleased, too, as long as I returned home for dinner and didn't stay out after midnight. My spirits were high, and they were content that I wasn't hiding under the covers all summer long.

Alexander seemed happier, too—and inspired. When we weren't roaming the cemetery at night, he painted landscapes and portraits of me. He began to churn out one beauty after another. Many of them were upbeat pictures of places around town we'd visited. The golf course, Dullsville High, Oakley Park, Hatsy's Diner, the swings at Evans Park, and the historic library. These paintings were bright and vivid and sweet and reflected his fondness for the town. I knew he had truly found his home here.

But unbeknownst to Alexander and me, all that was about to be changed by the letter that awaited him under the glow of the Mansion's lights.

Alexander took my hand in his as we left the Mansion and strolled down its drive. When we reached the gate, he drew me close.

"These last few weeks have been great. This is how it should always be. Just you and me."

"For eternity?" I asked, and stared up at him.

His hair hung sexily over his soulful eyes. There was a contentment I hadn't seen in Alexander. He gave me a long, breathtaking, weak-knee-making kiss. When we finally broke apart, something alongside the mailbox caught a reflection from the streetlight. The mailbox flag was sticking up.

"Funny. Does the mailman deliver your post at night? I thought only I knew your true identity."

Alexander appeared puzzled, too.

"Jameson is diligent about bringing the mail in as soon as it arrives."

"Well, that couldn't have been later than noon," I said. "Maybe they made a special delivery."

"I'll get it later," Alexander resolved with a shrug and put his arm around my shoulder. "I'll walk you home first."

"Forget that," I said before he could lead me away. "Maybe it's an invite to a party. Or notification that you won a trip to London."

"Or it could be a batch of coupons for pizza."

I glared up at him.

"Well, we'll never know unless you open it," I said coyly.

Alexander paused. Then he reluctantly leaned against the rickety box. He reached his pale fingers out to open the lid when we were struck with a few drops of rain.

"That's funny. It's not supposed to rain until tomorrow," I said.

Alexander drew back the metal door. "Be my guest."

I stared into the rusty mailbox, which was as dark as any tomb.

I half expected to see a detached hand holding out a letter. This was, after all, a vampire's mailbox. But I saw nothing.

"Are you afraid? It won't bite. But I might," he said, tickling me in the side.

"You promise?" I giggled as a few more drops of rain tapped me on the head. I imagined I could get snapped by a bird protecting its young or a field mouse hoping for a snack. I took a deep breath and reached my black chipped finger-nailed hand into the dark box but felt only a spiderweb. I reached in farther, allowing my ashen palm to disappear until I couldn't even see my Eve L wristband. Then I felt something pointy.

"It's not a package," I said, yanking it out. I had grasped a single standard-size black envelope.

I held it toward the streetlight. The letter looked odd. First of all, there wasn't a stamp, or even a postmark. Perhaps I had been right about a fang-toothed flying mailman. In perfect beautiful silver calligraphy it read: MR. ALEXANDER STERLING.

As I handed the envelope to my boyfriend, a few sprinkles of rain hit the letter A and the ink began to run.

"Looks like I'll have to drive you home," he said resignedly.

Alexander tucked the letter into his jacket and took my hand and we raced up the mile-long driveway, escaping into the Mansion.

I stood in the foyer of the magnificent Mansion. Lavender wafted through the estate. A new portrait of me stared back, a substitute for one of the original portraits that once lined the hallway.

"There's no return address," I remarked, smoothing out my hair.

"I recognize the handwriting."

"Really? Then who is it from? A long-lost girlfriend?"

"No."

"Are you sure?"

"I'm sure."

"I bet you get millions of love letters from old girlfriends."

Alexander placed the envelope on a hallway table. "Wait here while I ask Jameson for his car keys."

"Aren't you going to open the letter?"

"Eventually."

Alexander was patient and disinterested. I was neither.

"You must tell me who it's from," I said, snatching his mail. "Or *I'll* open it," I teased.

Alexander paused. "It's from my parents."

"Really?" I asked, surprised.

It had been ages since Alexander's parents had been to Dullsville, and Alexander rarely spoke of them. Most of the time, I forgot they existed.

"Well, open it up," I pushed, handing it back to him. "Maybe they sent you a check."

Alexander took a white gold **S**-shaped letter opener lying on the hall table. Unlike me, who ripped open mail like a wild animal, Alexander carefully severed the envelope.

He opened the black letter, which had a bloodred border. A check didn't fall out. Not even a Romanian leu.

Alexander began to read the letter to himself.

"What does it say?" I asked, bouncing around him and desperately trying to take a peek. But all I could make out was regal-looking letterhead with an inscription I couldn't decipher.

Alexander playfully held the letter out of my sight. But when he finished reading, he turned serious.

"What does it say?" I asked again.

Without answering, he put the letter in the envelope and returned it to the table. "I'll take you home now."

"What does it say?" I repeated.

"Nothing really."

"Your parents wrote to tell you nothing?"

"Uh-huh."

"Is everyone okay?"

"Yes."

"So why aren't you smiling?"

Then I thought maybe reading a handwritten note from them made him homesick. A creepy but kind butler wasn't a substitute for parents in a lonely old estate.

"I'm sure you miss them. I bet you wish you could see them soon."

"I will," he said. "They're arriving tomorrow."

"Tomorrow?" I asked, shocked.

"Yes," Alexander said, almost melancholy. That means

things are about to change."

I glanced around the Mansion. We felt like two teens who'd trashed the house with a party only to find their parents were returning from their vacation early.

"Our 'coffin clutches' will have to end," I said.

Alexander nodded reluctantly.

"And my decorations will have to be removed."

"It looks that way."

"What about my drawer?"

"I found the dresser key," he said with a smile.

As Alexander closed the door behind us, I managed to catch a last glimpse of the black rose petals lying on the hallway table. The painting of me would have to be shelved and the original ones returned. The votives would have to be stored away.

One thing was for sure: This time Alexander, not Jameson, would have to clean up the Mansion.

That night, I was torn as I sat cross-legged on my bean-bag chair watching reruns of *The Munsters*. Though I was anxious to finally meet Alexander's parents, I was sad the black lace curtains were being closed on our independence.

I'd never felt more at home than I did hanging out in the Mansion with Alexander over the summer. It was a dream come true to get a taste of the vampire lifestyle. Waking up at sunset, celebrating the darkness, living by candlelight. I was certain I could exist that way for an eternity.

But our summer of love was about to end.

Alexander was right. Things were about to change. His parents would be arriving shortly, and I'd be returning to school in a few days. No more late nights, no more remodeling the Mansion. Studying would replace painting, and I'd be home with my parents, Alexander with his.

I switched off my TV and joined my own odd relatives downstairs in our family room. My mom was folding laundry, and my dad was filing work papers. Typical suburban parents. The exact opposite, I was sure, of Alexander's. I wondered what Alexander's parents were like. Were they ghoulishly great like Herman and Lily Munster? I recalled stories of Dullsvillian sightings of the Sterlings when they first moved to town, but I'd never caught a glimpse.

I was sure they had to be fantastic—everything my parents were not. Reading the *Transylvanian Times* instead of Dullsville's *Ledger*. Changing into bats instead of plaid golf pants. Resting in a coffin instead of a sleigh bed. I bet they were the coolest parents in the world—or Underworld.

"I'm finally going to meet Alexander's parents!" I burst out to Becky the next day at Hatsy's Diner. When I slunk into the booth, Becky was flipping through the tabletop jukebox and sipping a strawberry malt. A chocolate one was kindly waiting for me.

Since summer began, Becky and I had both spent time with our true loves and not as much with each other. Though I did see her occasionally, we weren't as glued together as we'd been during past summers. I would have resented our separation if I didn't have a boyfriend, too. But since we were both guilty of trading lipstick for lip locks, it made it all right. I still missed my best friend and was excited to make up for lost time. I was in desperate need of some girl talk.

"Since I met Alexander, he's been parent-free. I'm not

sure how this will change our relationship," I explained to Becky.

"Maybe it will make it better."

"How? We had the whole run of the Mansion. I'm sure his mother wouldn't have approved of me being its interior designer."

"I'm sure they will be just fine."

"What if they're really strict and Alexander can't go out at night?"

"I can't imagine that," Becky said. "He lives for the night!"

"He'll probably have to do family things now."

"And chores," she added. "Matt has to constantly cut the grass. I grew up on a farm—obviously I know way more than he does about a lawn mower. But I act dumb as I watch him try to figure out how to put gas in it. Then I jump in and I'm all Bob Vila."

"Jameson does the chores. But cutting the grass? I think they add poison to the soil." We both laughed. "Besides, Alexander is responsible. He isn't like me in that way; he doesn't need to be nagged."

"I think you're worrying for nothing. I'm sure you'll all get along."

I slurped on my chocolate malt and stared off. "I wonder if Alexander looks like his mother or his father."

"Haven't you seen a picture?"

No. They are vampires! I wanted to say. In fact, the only images I'd seen were a few portraits Alexander had painted.

There were no family albums, no screen savers, no frames on the mantel.

"It's different in person," I said instead. "One thing is certain—I'm sure they are way cooler than my parents."

So many things were still new to me—having a boy-friend, discovering he was a vampire, and now meeting his vampire parents. I wondered how I'd fare.

I had always prided myself on being the one to give advice to Becky, but this time she was the experienced one.

"Isn't it strange when Matt's family is around?" I asked.

"Totally. He's a different person. No PDA. No holding hands. He even sits in his own chair instead of next to me on the sofa."

"That's what I'm afraid of. An end to my love life."

"You just have to make up for it when they aren't home. Or save it for school. But Alexander doesn't go to school. . . ."

"Don't remind me."

"So in your case plan more dates at the cemetery."

"What was it like when you first met Matt's parents?" I asked.

"I thought it would be fancy—like meeting them at the country club. Instead I was hanging out in Matt's fam-ily room when his mom came home from work. He said, 'Hey, Mom, this is Becky.' And she said, 'Hi, Becky, nice to meet you.' Then she disappeared. And it was pretty much the same with his father. It was different when Matt came to my house," Becky rambled on. "My mom made him sit down in the kitchen and she baked him a whole apple pie. I was so embarrassed."

"Yes, I remember you telling me that. But how did you *feel* with Matt's parents?"

"I was so nervous. I thought since I don't live in the 'burbs that they'd view me as this unkempt farm girl. But they are always happy to see me. I'm still waiting for them to give me my walking papers."

I stopped slurping my malt. I didn't live in a Mansion. And more important, I wasn't a vampire. I'd been so focused on how Alexander said things would change. Maybe he was alluding to more than a few pewter vases. Maybe he meant *me*.

"What if they don't accept me?" I blurted out.

"Why wouldn't they accept you?"

"I'm not like them."

"What do you mean?"

"I'm not . . ."

"Yes?"

I'm not a vampire! I'm a mortal. I'm not even like Luna Maxwell, who came from a vampire family. In Romania, Alexander had an arranged covenant ceremony with her, but since he wasn't in love with her, he couldn't go through with it.

"You're not what?" Becky asked.

"I'm not from Romania!"

"Duh," she said. "I think they know that."

"But maybe they want their son to date someone from Romania."

"Why would they want that when they live here?"

Because a girl from Romania would be like them, instead of like . . . us, I wanted to say.

"Listen, his grandmother built a mansion here. If Romania was so great, why would she move to this town?"

"But his grandmother was a baroness. My grandmother is a retiree."

"Alexander doesn't remind me of the snobby type. In fact, just the opposite. He's an outsider like . . ."

"Me?"

"Well . . . us," Becky admitted.

Maybe Becky was right. But I wasn't so easily convinced. I wasn't just from the wrong side of the tracks, I was from a different world.

Becky tapped her fork against my malt.

"Don't worry. Alexander is in love with you. That's all that matters. When Mr. and Mrs. Sterling see how happy he is, they'll be happy, too."

I smiled at my best friend's words.

"See, this is why we need to hang out together more," I said. "We can't let our boyfriends get in the way of our schedules—as hot as they may be."

"Well, we'll get to see each other every day now that school will be starting."

"Don't remind me. Summer is over."

"Can you believe we'll be juniors?" she asked like

she'd won the lottery.

Becky was lucky. She had an interest in school. Her best friend and boyfriend were by her side. I would have been excited to go back to school, too, if I were going to be seeing Alexander instead of my lifelong nuisance, Trevor Mitchell.

T he night before school started, I was stroking my kitten, Nightmare, and surfing the Net when she began to glare at my window and hiss. Her back arched and her fur stood straight up. I couldn't contain her in my arms. She bolted across my bed and jumped on the windowsill. She batted the glass with her paw.

"It's probably a bird, Nightmare. Calm down."

Then I heard a tiny *ping*, like something had hit the outside glass. Nightmare freaked. She dashed across my room and pushed through the cracked open door.

I peeked out into the darkness. It took a moment for my eyes to adjust.

I didn't see anything unusual around the garage or the swing set that was a few yards away.

But a shadowy figure was leaning against the tree. I pressed my face to the window.

There he was. My Gothic Guy, my Knight of the Night, my Vampire Prince.

My heart throbbed.

I raced out of my room, down the stairs, out the back door, and into my boyfriend's arms.

Alexander greeted me with a long kiss. It sent shivers down my spine.

"I had to see you," he said. "I can't stay long but I wanted to wish you luck before school."

"I've missed you so much."

"Me, too. I think even the Mansion misses you."

"How are your parents?"

"Fine."

"What are they like?" I probed.

"I don't know. . . . The same as any others."

"Are they happy to be home?"

"My mom says the Mansion smells like flowers."

"Did you tell her I placed them around?" I asked.

"I think she guessed."

"I bet you're glad to see them."

Alexander shrugged his shoulders.

"It's okay—I know you had to have missed them."

He hesitated and then began as if he were revealing a national secret. "It's been great to talk to my dad. He's an art dealer. He's very interesting and has so much to share about the art world. He brought me a painting from a rising artist in France."

"Does he like your artwork?"

"I'm not sure he takes me seriously yet. He thinks I just paint for fun."

"And your mom?"

Alexander's eyes couldn't help but twinkle.

"I bet she dotes on you," I said.

"She's my mom. She's insisting that I haven't eaten and has promised to fatten me up."

"When will I meet them?"

"Hopefully soon."

"I think you're hiding me."

"It's true . . . I want you all to myself." He squeezed me hard and swung me around.

"Do they know everything?"

"I don't tell my parents *everything*. Do you?"

Alexander had a point. I certainly didn't tell my parents that we had dates in the cemetery and I slept during the day with him in a coffin.

"Do they know I'm not a vampire?" I asked.

"Do your parents know I *am* one?"

I was shocked. Did Alexander have to hide my identity like I had to hide his? I thought maybe they knew already or they'd gotten wind of it from Jameson or the Maxwells. But either Jagger and his siblings, Luna and Valentine, hadn't returned to Romania or they hadn't wanted to share that Alexander had preferred a mortal to Luna.

And maybe Alexander chose not to tell his parents that I was mortal—like I'd chosen not to tell mine that he was a vampire. It didn't occur to me that he couldn't tell them the truth about me. I never realized how painful it must be for him that I couldn't disclose his reality to my parents or even my best friend.

"You don't want me to meet them, do you?" I asked. "Then they'll know."

"What?"

"You are ashamed of me."

"Why would I be ashamed?"

"That I'm mortal."

"All they know is that I have a girlfriend and that I'm happy."

I wasn't mad at Alexander. How could I be angry with him, when I hadn't shared him with my family, who I saw every day and he hadn't seen his in months?

But I was disappointed. I assumed Alexander would have told his parents every detail about finding the girl of his dreams in Dullsville and our adventures. But then, Alexander was a guy. I knew Billy Boy hadn't shared with my mom any crush he'd had on a very unlucky girl. I couldn't imagine Trevor spilling his guts about every girl he dated to Mrs. Mitchell—though he probably told the entire soccer team. Not only didn't Alexander talk to his parents, but he didn't have a friend in Dullsville besides me.

I felt a pang of loneliness for Alexander. He didn't have anyone to share his thoughts with. I guess that's why he spent so much of his waking hours painting.

Instead of being impatient as I normally was, I knew I needed to give Alexander space to reunite with his family.

"I have to go now. But I wanted to say hi," he said suddenly.

"I wish you could come to school with me tomorrow. I might be more motivated to get a better education if you were in my classes. Especially if I got to pass you in the hallway for a quick kiss."

"How about this to keep you company, since I can't be there with you?" He reached into his pocket and pulled out a dark-stained wooden bracelet with a dangling silver heart.

"I love it!" I said, putting it on.

Alexander gave me a long squeeze and a tender good-night kiss.

"When will I see you?" I asked, wrapping my arms around his waist like a giant handcuff.

"Sooner than you think." He gently pried my hands apart, stepped into the shadows, and disappeared.

Alexander was still a mystery. I ached to know everything about him, and his evasiveness only made me want him more.

4

Monster High

Most people fear the dark, afraid of the unknown—unsure what curious creatures might be hiding in their bedroom closets or on deserted streets. I embraced the night. It was the daylight I dreaded. I could *see* the monsters—and they all went to Dullsville High.

This year I'd be entering school a little differently than in the past. Not only would I be a junior, but this would be the first time I was returning to Dullsville High with a boyfriend. Plus I had knowledge of a vampire world and had many nocturnal adventures under my studded belt. But one thing hadn't changed: I was late.

The bell had already rung when Becky and I parked her truck. Suntanned students were scampering to class. I still hadn't adjusted to the early-morning school schedule. My stomach was churning and my eyelids hung heavy. Becky eagerly raced ahead of me as I climbed up the school steps like a zombie.

"Hurry," she said, diligently holding her books and class schedule at the front entrance.

It was then I realized I was missing some valuable information.

"Where's my schedule?" I ransacked my *Corpse Bride* purse, safety-pinned jeans pockets, and my backpack. Becky grew fidgety.

We had requested the same classes, but we had only gotten a few. And I didn't remember which ones.

"I know I have English first bell," I said, straining to remember. But I hadn't checked the schedule since summer break. "I think I might have Spanish second bell and third bell gym."

"We'll be late to them all!" Becky's face flushed red. Panic grew in her big brown eyes.

The sound of lockers shutting and classroom doors closing echoed off the hallway walls.

"Go ahead. I don't want us both to get suspended on the first day," I teased.

Relieved, Becky hurried to Mrs. Naper's English class while I proceeded back to the school's main entrance.

I plopped my backpack on the registrar's desk. The administrators were bright and perky, fresh from the glow of the summer sun and a few months sans students.

"Wow, classes haven't even begun and you're already in the principal's office," I heard a man's voice say as he came through the door behind me. "That's a first for you, isn't it?"

I turned around. Principal Reed, like me, was holding a cup of store-bought coffee.

I found his joke only halfway amusing, which made our school leader chuckle.

"How was your summer?" he asked, and noticed my blindingly pale skin. "Not much for the outdoors?"

I barely cracked a smile.

"You'd better get to class," he said. "Whichever one that is." He shook his head as he entered his office.

The school registrar asked me a few questions and then printed my schedule from her computer.

"I still have those nightmares," the registrar said. "Showing up to school without knowing what classes I'm taking or where the classrooms are located. The worst one was showing up for exams I hadn't studied for."

"One person's nightmares are another person's reality," I said. I took my schedule, gulped some coffee, and apathetically headed for class.

Mrs. Naper, a wiry woman with a mind bent on classics—and the tenure to prove it—greeted me with a stern glare and a few verbal admonishments. She was known throughout the Dullsville school system for the "Naper Paper," a college preparatory essay all juniors were required to complete, graded under the strictest of standards. Several things were in my favor, though. There was an empty seat next to Becky, and Trevor Mitchell was nowhere in sight.

"'To reiterate," Mrs. Naper began as I took a seat, "your

guidance counselor will be in to talk to you next month about college applications, scholarships, and grants. To prepare, your first assignment is a classmate interview and essay, followed by a brief presentation. Now that you are juniors you should be contemplating college and possible career paths. This essay will help stimulate you into discovering what you might like to pursue, and at the same time you'll get to know more about your classmates."

The Naper Paper actually sounded like a cinch to do. I knew everything about Becky, and likewise, she knew everything about me. We could complete the essay within the amount of time it took to type three hundred words and click SPELL CHECK.

"Raven," she continued, "while you were making your way to class, we assigned you a partner."

I turned to Becky. "Thanks for saving me."

My best friend averted her gaze away from me.

"What, you picked someone else?" I pressed.

"Someone else picked *me*." Then she pointed to a student in the front row. It was Matt.

"Ugh." I sighed. I felt as double-crossed as Charlie Brown when Lucy pulls the football away from him.

The classroom door opened and in walked Trevor Mitchell holding several boxes of chalk.

"Thank you, Trevor," Mrs. Naper said, her cheeks blushing as red as her lipstick as she took the chalk from the handsome jock.

"He's in this class?" I asked Becky. "I should have changed my schedule while I had the chance!"

My nemesis checked me out as he sauntered down the aisle toward me. When he reached my desk, he leaned in. "Hi, *partner*," he said with a wink.

My heart fell to the cold Masonite floor.

"Say it isn't so!"

I envied my best friend. She was assigned to her boyfriend and I was going to be stuck with Trevor. Forced to ask him questions that I didn't care to know the answers to. And in return, he'd pry into my private life. Why couldn't I be like Becky and have a boyfriend who attended school with me during the day, instead of being homeschooled at night? Though I'd dreamed of dating a vampire, it sure had its dark side. For a moment, I resented the whole nocturnal thing.

And even worse, I was going to have face time with Trevor Mitchell. I should just surrender my grade to Mrs. Naper and accept my F now.

"So remember," Mrs. Naper continued. "Junior-year grades are important. It's time to start thinking about your future. It's important that you take this assignment seriously."

Great. Not only has Trevor tormented me since kindergarten, but now, if I failed this assignment, he could screw up my whole future.

I made a quick escape from Trevor after the bell rang, but I wasn't so lucky at lunch. I was lying in the grass, shaded from the blazing sun by my sunglasses and a maple tree, when I sensed someone next to me.

I could smell the inviting aroma of just-cooked french fries.

"Hey, Becky," I said, undisturbed. "Did you bring me my fries?"

"No, but I brought you something else, Monster Girl," I heard a male's voice say. "Me."

I yanked off my shades. Trevor was stretched out next to me, resting on his elbow.

"Get away," I ordered.

"I figured this was a good position to start off the interview part of the assignment in," he said. "I can guarantee that you get an A. He held a fry in front of my lips, as if about to feed me.

I batted it away and the greasy fry flew out of his hand. "I can guarantee that you never see the light of day again."

He leaned into me, his blond locks only inches from my jet-black ones. "I want to explore all sides of you."

I almost gagged at his cheesy pick-up line and wedged my combat boot between us.

But he only took that as a sign of passion and held on to my shoe. "I knew you'd miss me. It's been all summer since I've seen you. I thought maybe you moved."

"I should have."

I yanked my foot away from him and scooted back. His fries spilled onto the grass, but he wasn't bothered. Trevor could buy the whole cafeteria if he wanted.

"Just think," he said. "You could have spent the summer with me, relaxing by the beach, rather than tending to a bat's nest. But you never did have good taste."

Matt and Becky approached carrying two sandwiches and holding my fries.

Since the Snow Ball dance where Trevor was outed as the one spreading rumors about Alexander's family being vampires and Matt began dating Becky, the soccer-snob twosome's relationship had become strained. They weren't the best buds they used to be, but Matt and Trevor acknowledged each other.

"Trevor was just leaving," I said. My nemesis rose and brushed off the dirt my boot had left on his freshly laundered designer polo shirt.

"So we're on for tonight, partner?" Trevor asked. "You can pick me up after practice. We don't want to wait until the last minute to begin."

Trevor snatched a bag of fries from Becky. "I believe these are mine."

Matt stepped before him, but Becky held him back.

"It's going to be a long year," I said resignedly, and flipped my shades back on my head.

I barely spoke as Becky drove me home. Each of my classes was more miserable than the last. My thoughts weren't on history or mathematical equations but on a vampire on Benson Hill. As we made our way home, Alexander was still safely tucked away in his attic room, unaware of anything going on in my world. It was strange that so much was happening and he wouldn't be able to find out until the sun set. I really wanted to be a part of his life—not just for the summer, but forever. I gazed out the window as we passed Dullsville's cemetery. So many romantic dates Alexander and I had spent on sacred ground. Why wouldn't I change my world for his? If only Alexander would bite me, plunge his fangs into my neck and draw out my sweet blood. It would mean an end to school and Trevor. And a new beginning for us.

That night, I danced on my front steps in wild anticipation of Alexander's arrival. I could almost smell his Drakkar and feel the soft skin of his cheeks against mine, his fingers sliding up the back of my spine, and his leg touching mine as we sat on the stoop. But after ten minutes had vanished like the setting sun, I began to pace. I was desperately waiting to jump into his arms and tell him about my horrible situation at school. He'd insist I was overreacting and my circumstances would right themselves before I knew it. I had taken care of myself for years, and this case was no different except for one major thing: I had a hunky boyfriend in my corner. I had someone to watch my back—even if that person was sequestered in a coffin. He'd laugh off the whole Trevor thing and threaten to turn my nemesis into dust if he so much as looked at me wrong.

Instead of hearing the twigs snap as Alexander emerged from the shadows, I heard the ringing of my cell phone.

"I won't be able to make it," Alexander said flatly.

"You're kidding . . ."

"My parents want to talk to me."

"Well, so do I."

"I guess that will have to wait. I promise I'll make it up to you."

"How's the drawer?"

"Everything is still intact. But I'd rather be holding you than your hoodies."

I didn't even have a chance to tell Alexander about the class schedule mixup, much less my run-in with Trevor.

I heard Jameson calling for him in the background, so my knight in shining Doc Martens had to hang up.

My evening schedule was making me as miserable as my daytime one.

5

Risk

I was feeling all doom and gloom—and not in a good way. I'd been stood up by my own boyfriend—the most dependable gentleman I knew. So I thought I'd find comfort in the only other man I could count on: my father.

Billy and my dad were playing Risk in the family room and fighting for global domination while my mom was laboring at the family computer.

"I thought you were going to meet Alexander," my mom said.

"I did, too," I said. I peered over my mother's shoulder. She was designing flyers for Dullville's Annual Art Auction.

I plopped down on the La-Z-Boy.

"How was school?" my dad wondered.

"The pits," I said. "I have a partnered English assignment and it's with Trevor. Matt picked Becky, and Trevor deliberately picked me. His sole mission in this world is to ruin my life. I'm not going to get into any college. I'll be forced to live here for the rest of my life."

My parents looked at each other in horror. The thought of a thirty-year-old gothic slacker running to raves and getting tattoos instead of jobs wasn't what they had planned. It didn't fit with their golf-outings-and-mixed-doubles-filled retirement plans.

"Why can't I be homeschooled like Alexander?" I whined.

"I think I saw Alexander's parents," Billy said suddenly.

"You did?" I asked. "You're not supposed to see them before I do!"

"Henry and I left Shirley's Bakery," he said, rolling dice, "and were cutting through the square when we spotted a lady and a man, dressed from head to toe in black, enter the Main Street Gallery."

I jumped up from my chair and faced my brother. "Did you see them up close?"

"I was too far away," he said, focused on his army. He was preparing to overtake Siberia. "But I'm sure it was them. No one in town is that ghost white. Their skin was so pale you could almost see through it."

"I'm looking forward to meeting them. I have to admit, I'm quite curious about them, too," my father said, moving his troops.

"You?" I asked. "What about me? Alexander hasn't even invited me over. There must be something wrong with me."

"Duh," Billy mumbled under his breath. "I've been telling you that for years."

I was gearing up to wipe out his Asian invasion when he covered his pieces with his scrawny body.

"You think it's me?" I asked my mother.

"Of course not. They just arrived in town. They're probably still settling in."

"I'm not so sure. . . . Something seems odd. Alexander never breaks dates."

"What happened to the confident girl I raised?" she asked. "You never cared what anyone thought of you. Not teachers, classmates, or even us."

My mom was right. But these people weren't regular people. These were the love of my life's parents. And they were vampires.

"Relax," my dad said as I started for my room. "Alexander's not keeping you a secret. Perhaps he's concerned about what you'll think of his *parents*."

I took my dad's words to heart. I had never thought of this situation from Alexander's perspective before. I remembered how embarrassed I was when Alexander first met my totally conservative mom and dad the night of the Snow Ball.

I surprised my dad and gave him a big hug. Though my dad was totally old school, at times like this he was the hippest guy on the planet.

6

A Walk in the Park

School days and nights passed by painfully slow sans Alexander. I tried to find comfort in Alexander's handmade bracelet, like a baby does a blanket. The wooden masterpiece remained wrapped around my wrist in the shower and during sleep, but it was no substitute for my boyfriend's arms.

I knew the Sterlings hadn't seen their son for so long; perhaps they wanted him all to themselves. I didn't know too many things about them, but that much his parents and I had in common.

It was as if I were seeing a mirage when I finally saw Alexander waiting for me at the Mansion's gate. However, he wasn't his usual loving self. He appeared distant and preoccupied, staring beyond me and off into the distance.

"Shall we go inside?" I asked.

"No—my parents are out and I'd like to get some fresh air, too."

Alexander walked, his hands in his pockets, kicking the fallen branches with his boots. I took Alexander's arm.

"I thought you'd be glad to see me."

"I am." He tried to perk up. "How's school?"

"I have this English project and it's with Trevor. It's to formulate our ideas about career paths, since we're supposed to start thinking about college."

"Do you know what you'd like to become?" he asked.

"I've known for years. But you'll need to help me a bit—or should I say, 'a bite.'"

"That's not really a career, though."

"Is a career that important?"

"To make money it is."

"You don't have to worry about that."

"Why would you say that?" he asked, stopping by an old maple tree.

"You live in a mansion. Duh."

"You think it's that easy?" he snapped. "That I can just buy whatever I want?"

I was taken aback. "I didn't mean to offend you."

"I don't have all the money in the world."

"I never said you did."

"That's not why . . . why you like me, is it?" The confident, content Alexander I'd seen a few days ago was nowhere in sight.

Something was troubling Alexander and I had to get to the root of it.

"What's wrong? You've never acted like this before. You really think I like you because you live in a mansion and have a butler? Besides, I don't like you—I love you."

Alexander shook his head. He took my hands and drew me near.

"So many things have changed so quickly. I just have to get things sorted out."

"You don't have to save the world every day, you know."

"We aren't going to be spending the time together that we once did."

"I know. I'm trying to deal with it, too. I get lonely and miss you like crazy. But once your parents settle in, that will change. They'll get sick of you, like my parents get sick of me."

Alexander cracked a smile.

"Besides, we have time together now. I've been waiting all day to see you. Let's talk about us."

"Or not," he said, his bad mood slowly disappearing. "We can talk later."

He leaned against a tree outside the Mansion and kissed me.

"Let's have some fun," he said.

"Wasn't *that* fun? I thought it was."

Alexander led me to Evans Park. He chased me around the jungle gym until I almost fainted from exhaustion. Out of breath, I flopped down on my back and gazed up at the stars.

"I wish every night was like this."

"If they were, then we wouldn't appreciate it."

"Maybe so. But I'd like to live this way forever."

"On your back staring at the stars?"

"With you." I stroked Alexander's hair and he playfully kissed me. "It's not too late," I said.

"For what?"

"To make me like you."

"Why do you have to be like me? Why can't you be like you?"

"Fine, have it your way. I'll be boring and mortal for the rest of my life."

"You think that I find you boring because you're not a vampire?"

I sat up. "I'm not exciting. I can't fly and I don't sleep in a coffin and except for my clothes, I guess I'm pretty normal." I hated to admit it even to myself.

"You are far from normal—you are extraordinary. You're free thinking, spirited, adventurous, and sometimes even dangerous. Not to mention irresistibly sexy!"

"Flatter me more!" I said, and gave him a huge hug. "Imagine if I slept in your coffin every day—not just a few weeks during summer break."

"I think about it every time I close the lid."

I realized it was hard on Alexander, too. But he didn't complain. He kept his feelings to himself, and he seemed to dwell on the positive, not brood on the negative, like I did. I still had a lot to learn from my vampire-mate, Alexander Sterling.

7

Sightings

"You'll never believe who I saw last night," Becky announced when she picked me up for school the following morning. I was fixing the indigo blue liquid eyeliner that I had accidentally smudged around my bag-ridden eyes. I was a vision of a true insomniac. Maybe there were advantages to not seeing one's own reflection.

Becky followed me into my bedroom and I grabbed my backpack.

"I saw Alexander's parents," Becky finally blurted out.

Her words were like an electric shock. Suddenly I was wide awake.

"You did?" I asked. "I still haven't seen them!"

"I know, it was so weird."

"What did they look like?"

"I really didn't see them up close."

"Then how did you know it was them? It might have

been a couple wearing dark clothes," I rationalized.

"Because I saw Jameson helping them out of the Mercedes."

"Wow! Then you *did* see them. Tell me everything!"

"I was driving Matt home from practice when we passed by the Emerson office building. The Mercedes was parked in front. Jameson opened the car door and a tall man in a cape stepped out with a lanky woman carrying an open umbrella. It wasn't raining. And even stranger, it was dark."

"It was them!" I deduced as we headed out the door. "It had to have been."

"Who carries an open umbrella at night under a perfect sky?" Becky asked.

"Only the coolest people in the world!"

The Emerson office building was a brand-new ten-story monolith. Businesses that once occupied the quaint and charming main square now inhabited the uncreative and antiseptic space. It was filled with everything from real estate to taxes. There was even a hair salon and a plastic surgery practice.

"Curious. I wonder what they were doing there," I said.

"Do you think Mrs. Sterling is getting a quick nip and tuck?" Becky asked.

"I don't think she'd need it."

"Maybe it's nothing more than boring tax advice," Becky offered when we got inside her truck.

"So they're going out of the Mansion. And for some

reason, I'm not going in. This calls for a Raven Madison—style investigation."

I passed the school day away waiting for the final bell to ring and wondering why the Sterlings were checking out the Emerson at night.

8 Atomic Spies

With the promise of a piping-hot Hatsy's burger and atomic fries, I bribed Becky into driving me to the Emerson building on our way home from school. It was like me to snoop, so I took advantage of my true nature. Of course, Becky was horrified with the whole idea and decided to wait in the car.

"I need your help," I said.

"You do so well on your own."

"We can cover more terrain with two people. I want to know what they might have come here for."

"Isn't that spying? Maybe Alexander's father was getting a haircut. Why would that be such a big deal?"

It wouldn't be if they weren't vampires, I wanted to say. "Nothing about them is usual."

Becky put the truck in park.

"Fine, I'll go myself. But leave the truck running in

1

case I need a quick getaway."

"Wait," she said, hopping out of the truck. "I'd better keep my eye on you."

"Works every time," I mumbled.

The Emerson building was like any other upscale office center. The blue and white glass structure was box-shaped. A three-tiered fountain highlighted the center of the building, and its Masonite floors sparkled as if they'd just been waxed.

Becky appeared to be intimidated by what she thought was a security guard ready to arrest all teen loiterers.

"It's an info desk," I said. "Chill out."

I made my way to the elevators and scanned the alphabetized list of tenants hanging on the wall.

"Now we have to see which one they went into."

"I thought you just wanted to know what was in the building."

I ignored Becky's comment. "They visited at night, so that should eliminate some of these."

I dragged Becky into the male-only hair salon.

"We only do men's hair," the overdyed red-haired receptionist said before I asked her a question.

"I know. Did a couple come in last night?"

"A male couple?"

"No, a man and a woman. They're from Romania."

"No."

"Well, thanks for your help," I said. "One down, five hundred to go."

We opened the glass doors to a Younger You cosmetic surgery office.

"Do you remember seeing a couple here yesterday?" I asked the receptionist, who could have doubled as a nurse.

"Our client list is confidential."

"I understand you can't tell me who visited your office, but you surely can tell me who didn't. So can you confirm that a man and woman from Romania *didn't* visit this office yesterday?"

She rolled her eyes. "Yes."

"Yes, they did?"

"Yes, they didn't."

Becky was getting fed up. Not with the office workers—but with me.

"How about I wait here?" she asked, pointing to the fountain.

"Just stay with me. I won't appear to be such a crackpot if you're by my side," I begged her.

We got in the elevator and made our way floor by floor, office by office. "Did a couple come in here last evening dressed like me?" I'd ask, and each receptionist would gawk at me and respond similarly. "No. I think I'd remember."

The last office was Berkley Realtors.

"I'm tired. Please, let's go home," Becky pleaded.

"But we only have one more to go."

"I'm leaving," Becky said, exhausted.

My feet hurt, too. And who knew, maybe one of these receptionists we spoke with wasn't working yesterday.

"All right," I said, guiding my weary friend into the elevator. "Enough parent hunting for today. . . ."

"Tomorrow," Becky said as the elevator doors closed, "you can take the bus."

Guess who my dad and I saw last night when we were out to dinner at Brios?" Trevor asked me the following day before class as I opened my locker.

"A cheerleader? A shopgirl? Or a teacher? You'll have to narrow it down. I can't keep up with who you are dating."

"The Sterling ghosts."

"No way." I dropped my backpack and faced him squarely. "You saw who?"

"Mr. and Mrs. Death. You'd better tell those morbid mannequins to go back to the dungeon they crawled out of. I was so repulsed I lost my appetite."

"Funny, you have the same effect on me."

"They're even freakier than you are. Are you sure you aren't their spawn, too?"

"What did they do? Who were they with?" I asked.

"Haven't you met them yet?" Trevor seemed as surprised as I had been.

"Of course. Several times." I picked up my backpack and began shoving textbooks into my locker.

"You haven't, have you? I guess I'm not the only one who thinks you are weird. Alexander does, too."

His comments were like a stake in my heart.

"They met someone," he continued. "Mr. Berkley came over to their table. I thought he might faint, but he didn't."

"Mr. Berkley of Berkley Realtors?" I then realized that his was the last suite in the Emerson building left to investigate.

"Rumor is that they want to buy the cemetery and move in."

I was fuming. Trevor had seen the Sterlings before I had. Plus, I was angered that he was ridiculing Alexander's mother and father.

"Maybe they want to buy your house and use your room for landfill," I countered.

My mind raced as to how the Sterlings were acquainted with Mr. Berkley. Was he who they really saw at the Emerson building? Were they planning on buying Jameson his own place now that they were home? I'm sure there was a plausible explanation for their encounter.

"Could you hear what they said?" I inquired.

"I think it was 'Can I borrow your blood?' How do I know what they said? So . . . when are we going to start our essays?"

When I see my boyfriend's parents, I wanted to say. Instead I slammed my locker shut and stormed off.

I'd been kept in the dark long enough.

Everyone in town seemed to have a Sterling parental unit sighting but me. I was going to make sure that all that changed. If the Sterlings weren't coming to me, I resolved, I'd go to them.

As the sun set, I took my RBI (Raven Bureau of Investigation) accessories: small backpack, flashlight, and compact mirror. Garlic powder was not necessary and in this case would repel instead of attract the objects of my investigation. It wasn't the first time I'd snuck onto the Mansion's property.

I knew the lawn and grounds better than I knew my own backyard. Still, there was one thing I hadn't counted on: The wrought-iron gate was locked. Alexander had been leaving it open, for my easy entrance. More had changed than I thought.

I was going to have to scale the fence. I reached and tugged and climbed my way up to the top like I was on a Mount Everest expedition. I guess sleeping in the coffin for all those weeks during the day didn't do anything for my upper body strength. But I persevered.

I kicked my foot over the top of the gate. A gargoyle stared at me.

I let go and dropped down with a thud.

The Mansion appeared to be empty. I was just about to sneak in when I heard a car pull up to the gate and park.

The gate was being unlocked.

I stole behind a bush.

The Mercedes drove through the entrance and up the winding driveway. It parked in front of the Mansion.

Jameson got out and two figures emerged from the car, followed by a third. Was it Alexander? It was so dark I couldn't make out my own boyfriend.

From a safe distance, I followed the shadowy figures as they made their way inside the estate, which became illuminated by candlelight, room by room.

Once again, I was alone. An outsider peering in. In Dullsville, at school, in my own family, and now with my boyfriend's family.

I saw Alexander's attic room light up. I assumed Alexander was painting or maybe dreaming of me as I was dreaming of him.

Two figures suddenly appeared at a window. I flung myself back into a bush against the gigantic house. I craned my neck and strained to see up to the second story. Two deadly pale faces peered out the curtainless window—like apparitions searching for something or someone they'd lost. The figures disappeared and the room went black.

I had seen Alexander's parents!

10
The Invitation

I coasted my way home and was parking my bike in the garage when I heard the sound of something hovering a few feet away from me. Cautiously I tiptoed toward the door, my flashlight primed for any maverick vampires.

I saw nothing. Just my dad's parked SUV. I was sure it was a hungry raccoon foraging for leftovers in our garbage can.

Then I heard a twig snap. And footsteps.

I decided to make a run for it. Our back door was only ten yards away from the garage. All I could think of was Freddy Krueger. Michael Myers. Or hockey-masked Jason. Crazy horror movie stalkers haunted my thoughts. I'd seen far too many scary movies to shake them from my mind. *Think kids shows*, I thought. *Barney. Teletubbies. Dora.* Those images frightened me more.

If I had my keys ready, I'd make it safely inside before anything could cause me bodily harm. I took a deep breath and geared up to charge forth. But before I took my first step, I was caught in a surprising trap. It wasn't Trevor blocking my escape in the shadow from the garage, or even the most nefarious vampire of all—Alexander's enemy, Jagger Maxwell. It was Alexander.

"Oh . . . It's just you. Thank goodness!" I made my way to hug him, but he kept his arms folded.

"Where were you?" he asked. He stood stern as my father had many times when I'd broken curfew.

"I just went out for a ride," I said truthfully.

"By yourself? At night?"

"It's still early. My bike has a light on it." All true.

"Then what's that for?" he asked, pointing to my flashlight. "Were you searching for something? Or rather some*one*?"

"It's always good to have extra light. I'm not like you: I can't see in the dark." I grimaced, hoping he'd grin back. His stony expression remained fixed.

"I went to your house," I confessed. "Everyone in Dullsville, including Matt, Becky, and Trevor, has spotted your parents. All I had was a vague memory of a portrait you'd painted of them. I wanted to see them for myself."

I felt awful. My impatience had gotten the best of me once again. I'm not sure how I'd feel if Alexander was sneaking around my house, trying to ogle my parents as if they were subjects in a sideshow. I was no better than the local gossipmongers.

I waited what seemed like an eternity for Alexander's response. I was so ashamed of myself I barely made eye contact.

My boyfriend took my wrist and gently drew me to him.

"I think I might have to place you under arrest for trespassing. But I always go easy on pretty girls who confess," he said ominously.

"You knew, didn't you? I'm that predictable?"

"It was just a matter of time before I spotted you hiding in our bushes."

"So you're not mad?"

"I'm not through with you yet. Are you prepared to accept your punishment?"

I nodded reluctantly. I wasn't sure what a vampire's punishment might be. But I was ready to find out.

"I sentence you to a thousand kisses," he said.

"Can I begin now?"

He finally smiled. I pressed my lips to his and snuggled against him.

When we broke away, I apologized again.

"It's okay. It's time that you meet them. But for tonight, you'll have to settle for me." Alexander winked.

And for the next hour I continued to fulfill my sentence.

* * *

Another letter arrived mysteriously—only this time it was at my house.

"You have mail," my mom said when I got home the following day. "It's on the kitchen table."

I wasn't used to receiving cards when it wasn't my birthday or a holiday. Even if it was a college brochure, I was excited something was addressed to me.

A deep purple envelope lay next to our pastel blue salt and pepper shakers.

In beautiful black calligraphy it read: *Miss Raven Madison.* Like Alexander's mail it was devoid of postmarks or stamps. On the back it had a candle-waxed pressed seal of an S.

I almost tore into it when I remembered how Alexander opened his mail.

"Mom," I called. "Do we have a letter opener?"

"I think there's one in your dad's desk."

I opened the French doors to my dad's office. He had a dark oak desk topped with family pictures. I scanned the desk for any sharp objects but didn't find anything other than a few pens and a golf tee. I was growing antsy and rifled through his desk drawer.

Finally, underneath a file folder, I found a gold letter opener, the end in the shape of a tennis racket. I carefully slit open the envelope.

I pulled out the note card and read:

Mr. and Mrs. Constantine Sterling
request the pleasure of your company
for dinner this Friday at sunset
The Sterling Mansion
Benson Hill

It was official. I was finally going to meet Alexander's parents, and I had the invitation to prove it!

11

Dress Code

What do I wear to meet parents?" I asked Becky in my bedroom later that day. "I don't have a thing! It's way different than trying to impress a guy. It has to be something striking yet appropriate."

"Hello! You have a whole wardrobe that screams mansionwear!"

"Really? You say the kindest things!" I exclaimed.

Becky was stretched out on my bed reading one of her teen mags while I mixed and matched several outfits and modeled them.

"They all look good to me."

"But I have to look great! This one is too sexy," I said, holding a black bodice. "And this one is too casual," I said, holding up a HIM T-shirt. "How am I going to pull it off? This could make or break my relationship with Alexander."

"This mag is full of great styles." Becky opened to a spread.

"For me? Are the girls modeling tattoos and tongue piercings?"

"I don't think so. But that doesn't mean it can't help inspire you."

"Alexander would drop dead if I showed up in a polka-dotted dress."

"Just give it your spin. If they're showing striped Keds sneakers—then choose skull and crossbones Vans."

It was great to have a best friend who understood me.

But the models were beautiful and glowing in their candy-colored outfits. I guess I couldn't hide my slight jealousy of their perfect bodies.

"Hey, everyone can be gorgeous with airbrushing," Becky remarked. "And we are fabulous without it!"

"You really expect me to put my hair in a ponytail with plaid ribbon?"

"No. You'd wear pigtails with an uneven part and black lace bows. Or better yet, Wednesday Addams braids."

"You are onto something. Maybe we could start our own magazine. Something where the models dress like me. *Gothicgirl*!"

"I'd buy it. I'd totally not wear anything in it, but I'd buy it," Becky assured me.

"I'll be the editor, and we could have articles about music and fashion and we'd interview Criss Angel," I said excitedly. "And in every issue I could be on the cover—like Oprah, but wearing all black."

"And Alexander, too," Becky added. "I bet every girl across the country would buy a copy."

"But he couldn't be on the cover."

"Why?"

"Uh . . ." I almost blurted out the true reason, but I caught myself. "Because it's my magazine. Not his. He'll have to get his own. How about *GQ. Gothic Quarterly*," I said, covering my tracks.

"Awesome! Now that we've decided on your career, we need to pick your outfit."

We matched a few outfits together and voted on them until only one was left. A black mini lace dress, black tights with knee-high boots, and a lace bodice.

"A marriage made in heaven—or in my case, hell."

We both laughed.

"Well, what do you think?" I asked.

"Drop-dead gorgeous!"

The first time I had a dinner date with Alexander I was nervous. Would he like me? Would he ask me out again? Would it end in a passionate kiss?

This dinner would be different. I brushed my hair a thousand times and reapplied my makeup. Was I too pale or not pale enough?

On this date I'd be judged by Alexander's parents. Would the Sterlings think I was a good fit for their son? I knew they had approved of Luna—but I wasn't Luna. I didn't come from Romania or have vampire blood or a vampire family. My whole relationship was riding on this one meal.

I was getting ready when my mom poked her head into my room.

"So, are you excited about your big night?" my mom asked.

I tried to downplay its importance and hide the panic attack I was having. "Sure, it's no big deal."

"Of course it is. You are going to meet your boyfriend's parents!"

"You are supposed to make me feel better—not worse!" I whined.

"That's not what I meant. I meant it is exciting."

I felt tears welling. Any minute my eyeliner was going to bleed down to my shoes.

"No—it's a make-it-or-break-it night. I'm not like them."

"Why do you have to be like them? You are you." My mom smiled.

"The Sterlings have royal blood. Alexander's grandmother was a baroness. I'm sure they've dined with kings, queens, and noblemen. They live in mansions! They are from Romania. I'm from Dullsville." I plopped down on my bed.

"Just relax."

"How can I relax? You have no idea what it's like."

"You don't think I do?" she asked, sitting down next to me. "Your father and I were both hippies, remember? Our parents were ultraconservative. When I first met Grandma

Madison, I was in a tank top and cutoffs. I'm surprised she ever let me in her house again."

"Really?"

"It's normal to be nervous. Think of how Alexander feels. He wants you to like them, too."

"You think he's anxious, too?"

"Of course he is. He probably thinks his parents will embarrass him, just like you think we will."

I felt relieved knowing that I wasn't carrying the entire burden of our meeting.

"I'm sure as soon as the Sterlings meet you," my mom continued, "they'll love you like I do."

"You have to love me; you're my mother." I rolled my eyes.

"Let's see what you chose to wear."

"Are you kidding? Becky and I already decided on it. I can't go back now."

"I'm sure you chose something appropriate. I'll go downstairs until you're ready."

I retouched, rebrushed, and fussed until my Edward Scissorhands clock flashed, "You're late!"

I flew down the stairs to find my family hanging out in front of the TV. I modeled my outfit.

"Shouldn't you wear something more...conservative?" my mother asked. "How about a pretty knit sweater?"

I ignored my mother's remarks.

"You look wonderful," my dad said.

"I think she looks awesome," I heard Henry say to Billy Boy.

"I think I'm going to hurl," my brother retorted.

I hugged my parents exceptionally hard. I was going to be dining with adult vampires. Who knows—I might never come back.

A few minutes later our doorbell rang.

I was too nervous to answer, so Billy Boy opened the door.

"One moment," he said in his politest voice. "Raven— it's for you."

I took a deep breath and started for the door. Jameson stood before me, complete in his butler's uniform and gloves. "Miss Raven, your car awaits you."

My mom winked and my dad gave me a thumbs-up.

As Jameson and I walked down the driveway, I glanced back. Billy Boy and Henry were spying through the front window. Then two more heads popped into view—former hippies Paul and Sarah Madison.

Jameson led me to the parked Mercedes and kindly opened the back door.

My parents were impressed with my chauffeur and gothic limo service, even if the chauffeur was unusually creepy.

12

Royal Blood

It seemed as if it took an hour for Jameson to drive me to the Mansion. I was afraid by the time we reached its gates, dinner would be stone cold.

We parked in front of the Mansion. It was quite the celestial sight. Candles flickered inside the house like a festive holiday party.

Jameson opened the car door for me.

I reached the top of the crumbling stairs, and, as if on cue, the front door creaked open. On the other side were the first adult vampires I would ever meet. At first I didn't see anyone. Then out stepped Alexander, stunning in an oversized blue silk shirt and black jeans.

"Wow! You are beautiful." He offered his hand to me and kissed me on the cheek.

Somber violin music faintly filled the Mansion. A pewter umbrella stand containing at least half a dozen parasols sat by the front door.

"Miss Raven is here," Jameson called to the second floor, and retreated to the kitchen.

"My mom takes forever."

The Mansion's air was unusually chilly, and I was shivering.

"Are you nervous?"

"Petrified. And cold."

"My mom likes the thermostat set to freezing. I'll fix that."

"That's okay—," I started to say.

But Alexander had already taken off.

A ghoulish and magnetically morbid woman descended the red velvet staircase like an apparition. Her perfectly straight jet black hair, streaked with a vivid violet, cascaded over her bony and beautiful shoulders.

She continued to come down the stairs, with the confidence of Cleopatra but the attire of Elvira. Deep eggplant-hued lipstick and nails were ghastly and gorgeous against her corpse-white skin.

Strong black eyeliner intensified her blue catlike eyes, and her long, purple, flirty eyelashes sparkled. A tattoo of a black rose crept out from her dark velvet corset, which shaped her chest like a heart. Her small cinched-in waist was accentuated with a fabric belt and a long, flowing black mermaid skirt. Her frame was petite but curvy in all the important places.

I was mesmerized by her beauty.

At the end of the staircase a man appeared out of the

shadows. He was tall, with broad shoulders and blazing black and gray shoulder-length hair. He was utterly handsome, as striking as any fifties film star. His dark eyebrows were in sharp contrast to his frost-toned skin. He wore a dark silk suit with a bloodred tie and a matching cape. He had a sharp antique wood walking stick, capped with an ivory skull. Alexander's father formally took his wife's hand and led her toward me.

I froze. I was standing in front of Alexander's parents. I didn't know if I should bow or salute. To me, they were the most normal-looking parents I'd ever seen.

Mrs. Sterling extended her hand to me. In the most lyrical Romanian accent, she said, "It is our pleasure to meet you, Raven."

I couldn't help but notice the two purple bite marks on her neck.

I tried to speak, but I was so in awe. My words stuck in my throat.

Just then Alexander returned.

"This is Raven," he said proudly.

"We were just introducing ourselves," his mother stated.

"I'm so happy to meet you, Mrs. Sterling," I finally said.

Her hand was cold but firm. "Call me Cassandra."

"And this is my father, Constantine," Alexander said.

Mr. Sterling extended his hand to me. "It is lovely to meet you, Raven." His voice was deep, causing shivers to flow through my body. His dark eyes were intense and hypnotic.

"You are just as beautiful as Alexander described," the dashing senior Sterling complimented. "And he has exquisite taste." He grinned, and the candlelight caught the edge of his icicle-sharp fangs.

I wasn't sure if he meant "taste" literally. I was, after all, being greeted by a vampire.

"Alexander has told us so much about you," Mrs. Sterling said.

"He has?"

"Come, we'll be dining outside tonight. I'm bloodthirsty and starved to the bone."

We walked to a side door, where an umbrella was leaning against the wall.

"The moonlight can be so strong." Mrs. Sterling opened her umbrella and went down the back stairs. The violin music grew louder.

The backyard was grimly festive. Awaiting us was a grand gothic affair. A long black runner ran along the grass from the bottom of the steps to a morbid dinner party under the stars. Four torches burned, presumably to repel insects (but in this case, more likely, to attract them) several yards away from a long, dark wooden table. On closer inspection, I could see that a coffin lid had been transformed into a dining-room table. Several floor-length candelabras surrounded the table, wax dripping like trickling blood. Alexander offered me a chair and gently pushed it in for me as Mr. Sterling did the same for his wife. Mrs. Sterling sat at the head of the casket and Alexander's father at the end, while Alexander and I sat at the other sides.

I was surprised to see a string trio in the gazebo—two men dressed in tuxedos and a woman in an evening dress—playing in a minor key unmelodious funeral-type music. I didn't recognize the musicians as being from Dullsville. I had assumed the music was coming from an entertainment center. I had no idea it was being played live. Or rather, undead.

This was unbelievable. It was as if they had transformed the backyard into a cryptic dining hall. All that was missing was a china cabinet.

If Becky and my parents could see me now, they'd never believe I was at the center of this macabre dinner celebration. If only I could immortalize it with a photograph—but then again, most of the diners wouldn't come out.

Jameson quickly tended to Mrs. Sterling. He poured her a glass that appeared to be champagne mixed with blood.

"I like mine bubbly," she said with a laugh.

Jameson approached me with his Underworldly concoction. "I'll have a Coke," I said.

"Of course, Miss Raven."

Then Jameson attempted to serve Alexander, but my boyfriend covered his glass with his hand. "I'll have what Raven is having."

He finished by pouring Mr. Sterling a tall glass and, from a neighboring chest, retrieved two sodas.

"Let's toast," Mrs. Sterling said, raising her drink. "To Raven and Alexander—may your friendship last an eternity."

Friendship? I wondered. Hadn't Alexander told them we were dating? Or was she just being polite? I gazed at my boyfriend, who seemed distracted. Our glasses clinked underneath the twinkling stars.

"So how did you and Alexander meet, exactly? You know men can be so vague when it comes to details."

I snuck into your house and found him standing behind me, I wanted to say. *Or do I count Becky almost running your son over in the road outside the Mansion?*

"Uh . . . I . . ."

"I saw Raven several times before I had the courage to invite her here for dinner," Alexander answered for me.

"How romantic," Mrs. Sterling remarked. "A private dinner date. Mr. Sterling and I met at the cemetery."

"Wow—that's romantic, too," I said truthfully.

"We are so happy Alexander has found someone to keep company with," she said fondly.

"Mrs. Sterling and I understand that Alexander has told you about our family," Mr. Sterling said. "We'd expect a far different reaction from a girl in your situation and find not only your tolerance but your enthusiasm refreshing."

I didn't know what to say, so I remained silent.

"We find it very intriguing that you have the same passion for certain things that my mother did," he continued, gesturing toward his family. It seemed as if he was alluding to the Underworld without actually saying it. "Alexander shared her interest in painting, while you seem to share her other passion."

Vampires? They waited for my reaction. How was I supposed to respond? I turned to Alexander for help. His normally soulful eyes appeared to be red.

"I think we should talk about something else—," Alexander said to his father.

"I must say, it does concern Mrs. Sterling and me," Mr. Sterling continued. "My mother was a very lonely woman isolated in a town very different from her own family. I wouldn't want you to suffer that same fate."

Alexander was fuming. "We've invited Raven over for dinner, not a dissertation."

"Constantine, Alexander's right," Mrs. Sterling interjected. "There is plenty of time for such matters."

"Let's just say we appreciate your acceptance of our lifestyle and leave it at that," he said.

"So what do you enjoy doing?" he asked politely, changing the subject.

"I love to go to the cemetery, watch TV, and listen to music."

"How about school? Do you enjoy your studies?" Mr. Sterling wondered.

"Not much. I'd rather be homeschooled, like Alexander."

"Is there a subject you are attracted to? Something that you fancy becoming?" Mr. Sterling asked.

A vampire, I was dying to say. *Like all of you.* But I didn't have the guts.

"Raven has plenty of time for questioning," Mrs. Sterling said. "Let her eat."

Jameson came in with a tray of almost too fresh meat. It was about as unappetizing as it could be. I was really too nervous to eat anyway and figured I'd get my calories from the veggies.

Jameson handed me a special plate—a quarter chicken fully cooked.

"Are you sure you wouldn't prefer some of ours?" Mrs. Sterling asked. "There is plenty here."

"Raven prefers hers well done," Alexander responded.

"Be sure to try it this way. It's very addicting," Mrs. Sterling added.

It was then the candlelight caught the wounds of her bite marks.

Was being vampires something Alexander's parents had wanted? Or would they resist bringing me further into the vampire world than I already was?

We retired from the crisp night air of our backyard party to the chilly living room of the Mansion. Jameson brought in our desserts.

Above a small fireplace was a portrait of a dashing gentleman.

"That was my father," Mr. Sterling offered, noticing my stares.

"He was very handsome," I said.

Mr. Sterling laughed.

"He would have been pleased to know you thought so."

"This Mansion was built in honor of him," Mrs. Sterling began. "And used to its fullest. It's been a wonderful place for Alexander, too. He has accomplished a lot here."

"I'll say," I remarked. "He has painted so many paintings. You could decorate the Mansion with them," I went on.

"You've seen his artwork?" Mr. Sterling asked.

"Yes. He won an annual arts fair contest. Didn't Alexander tell you?"

"No, we didn't know that," Mr. Sterling said.

"Alexander, you are holding back on us," Mrs. Sterling said.

"It was a picture of me," I gloated, "and people said it was dead-on."

"Interesting," Mr. Sterling said. "So that is what you've been doing with your spare time?"

"He paints all the time. He's made dozens. Have you seen them?"

Alexander shook his head and signaled me to cut off this discussion.

"No, Alexander doesn't share his work with us," said Mr. Sterling.

"Well, why don't we bring some down?" I offered.

Suddenly there was ice in the air.

"Later," Alexander said. "Constantine is a very busy man. He's too preoccupied with professional artists. I'd rather not waste his time."

Constantine? Alexander called his father Constantine?

"But—"

"So, Raven," Mr. Sterling said, changing the subject. "Tell me about your parents."

"They are just like everyone else here in town." Then I realized I could be accentuating their mortality. "But they really like staying up late and they love the night. And my dad likes his steaks really rare. Growing up we watched

Dracula movies together. He loves vampires."

The three vampires looked straight at me. I had rambled on too far.

"I've finished my dessert now, Alexander," I said.

"It's time I take you home," Alexander responded right away.

Alexander held my hand as the Sterlings accompanied me to the door.

The ghoulish couple stood statuesque and imposing, yet mannerly.

"It was great to meet you," I said sincerely. "And thanks for dinner."

"Please give our regards to your parents," Mr. Sterling said, and gave me a polite kiss on the cheek. It was enough to make my frozen heart melt.

"Yes, we must meet them," Mrs. Sterling said. "We'll have Jameson set something up immediately."

Bad idea, I wanted to say. "I know they'd be honored," I uttered instead.

"What a sweet girl," Mrs. Sterling said. "I'd like to get to know you better, Raven," she remarked before I stepped out the door.

My eyes lit up. "Absolutely. I'm free any time."

The sight of Mrs. Sterling and I hanging out at the mall together would be sure to turn the town of Dullsville on its head. We'd probably show up on the local news.

13

Graveyard Glam

I never expected that I'd have a "girls' night" with Mrs. Sterling. Becky—always a given. My mom—when we both were in good moods. My aunt Libby—when I'd visit her in Hipsterville. But Mrs. Sterling? The mother of my true love? I couldn't have dreamed of this night, even with my outlandish overactive imagination. And it was about to take place.

I had to wonder what her motives might be. Was she trying to get the scoop on how I really felt about Alexander? Or was this a chance to get the scoop on me?

Either way, I didn't care. I was preparing to go out with the most fabulous, ghoulish mom on the planet. Everything was working out after all. I got to meet Alexander's parents, have some adult vampire time, and would soon get full reign of the Mansion again.

I parked my bike at the Mansion's gate at dusk and knocked on the door. Instead of being greeted by Alexander, Jameson bid me welcome.

"Hello, Miss Raven. Mrs. Sterling is looking forward to your visit. If you'll wait in the parlor room, she will be with you shortly."

I was leafing through *Romanian Castles* when I felt a presence at the doorway.

Mrs. Sterling, in a black floor-length V-neck dress and a lovely hat secured with a lavender lace scarf, extended her hand to me. Glistening jewels sparkled on her long medieval purple fingernails. "I've been waiting for a night like tonight for centuries."

"Me, too," I said.

"There is something I'd like to show you." She held out an antique photo album.

Jameson brought us a tray of drinks and set them on a side table. There was a tall red drink with a celery stick garnish and a Coke with an umbrella.

"You remind me so much of someone I know," she said in a sultry voice.

"Who?" I asked.

"Alexander's grandmother," she answered.

"Really?"

"Here's a picture of her." Mrs. Sterling opened the weathered photo album. "This is my husband's mother."

She showed me a picture of a thin woman with high

cheekbones and Alexander's soulful eyes.

Some of the pages were fraying away from the binding and a few pictures were coming unglued. "This Mansion meant everything to her. And so did her family. As you might know, she and Alexander's grandfather were barons. They kept company with heads of state and other royalty, such as kings and queens across Europe."

I knew it! She is going to tell me that I'm not of royal blood—therefore I'm not worthy of her son.

"But they escaped Romania," she continued, "when the family was being persecuted. She saved them, really. If it wasn't for her quick thinking, there would never have been a safe Constantine and never an Alexander. She kept the royal bloodline alive. And that is very important to all of us."

"Wow—she sounds very brave," I began to say.

"When it was safe, Constantine went back to Romania. His mother remained here."

I hung on her every word.

"Did Alexander tell you why he moved here?" she asked.

"Yes, but he may have left something out. He can be mysterious."

"Our family had an arrangement with the Maxwells— another prominent and noble family in Romania—with their daughter, Luna. We wanted to carry on our royal bloodline. It was very important to Mr. Sterling, you see. He's spent so much time worrying about his mother, isolated in this mansion, away from our own kind. He wanted someone for Alexander who would be like us—who would make us all happy. What we didn't realize was that on the big day the one person who mattered the most wasn't happy: Alexander.

"Luna was a fine girl and the Maxwells are a wonderful family. But when Alexander rejected them, it sent our world into chaos. The only safe haven was for Alexander to come here and live in the Mansion. Away from the Maxwells.

"My heart broke that day. Alexander has been so far away from me. And now that we have returned for him, there was something else we didn't plan on: You."

I didn't know what to say.

"I was a lot like you when I was your age."

"Were you an outsider?" I asked.

"Yes, and I dressed in wild outfits and danced at parties until sunrise."

I wondered what could be wilder than the attire she was already sporting.

"When I met Mr. Sterling everything fell into place. However, his mother was unlike all of us. She was courageous and regal—and mortal. I never could live up to her image. Mr. Sterling and Alexander think you are like her."

"Courageous?"

"Yes. And she was a true outsider. In her world and in ours. But she was hot-blooded about the Underworld. You have a passion for our world that *we* don't even have. And that you share with Alexander's grandmother.

"I just wanted you to know that by dating

Alexander—there are concerns we have. We wouldn't be responsible adults if we didn't look out for you—just as we would for our own son," she went on.

Do you want me to be turned? I wanted to say. *Just say the date.* But I knew it wasn't that simple. And Mrs. Sterling didn't appear to be heading down that path.

"Now, enough serious talk," she continued. "I'd like to have a little girl time."

"Fine by me."

"Are there any tattoo parlors?" she asked with a whimsical laugh.

"Not around here."

"Soothsayers?"

"A few towns over."

"Any snake charmers?"

"Only once a year, when the carnival comes to visit."

"Well then, we'll have to make our own fun," she said emphatically. "Jameson, get the car!"

I scooted into the Mercedes next to Mrs. Sterling, her umbrella resting between us as Jameson drove us to town.

"Stop here," Alexander's mother called to Jameson when we came to the town square. It took a few moments for the creepy man to react and press the brakes. We stepped out of the car and into the busy square.

Main Street was filled with upscale preppy boutiques. It was a hangout for families, dog walkers, and strolling seniors. Mrs. Sterling, poised with her umbrella, sunglasses, and purple velvet purse with black lace ribbons, was quite the sight to see. Even I found myself gawking at her. It was as if I were walking with a movie star. Dullsvillians, however, thought we were a freak show. Snickers and giggles and stares followed us up and down the block.

Mrs. Sterling, with her statuesque figure and graveyard-glam style, was oblivious to the stares. She looked like any A-list star, unfettered by her paparazzi.

When we passed a few people walking dogs, the animals became unruly. Mrs. Sterling didn't seem to even notice the upset pets.

We stopped in front of Purse Party. Mrs. Sterling was enamored by a leopard clutch purse in the window.

"Let's peek inside," she said.

We stepped into the overpriced boutique. The gimmick was you picked a purse style, fabric, buttons, and ribbons and walk away with a unique custom-made handbag. Long tables were set up in the middle of the store, with sample fabric strewn across haphazardly, as if there had just been a purse-picking party.

The owner had no idea who—or what—had just entered her shop. I could tell her face was straining, trying to hold back her real thoughts. She was ready to push the panic button. Instead she did her best to feign enthusiasm. "We specialize in one-of-a-kind purses. We can come to your home and if you have at least five women show up, you get a free purse."

I could just imagine the shopkeeper, swatches of fabric in tow, arriving to discover the Mansion instead of her usual five-bedroom cookie-cutter mega-mansions and speeding away before her tires passed the wrought-iron gates.

Mrs. Sterling didn't say a word as she cased the shop. She held her umbrella with one hand, and with her free one she picked through purses.

I sensed the saleswoman was checking her inner clock, hoping we'd get out of the store immediately.

"I'm absolutely crazy about this!" Mrs. Sterling exclaimed, holding up a woolly black carpet bag. "Do you have leopard print?"

"Yes. Would you like piping, trim, or ribbon?" the woman asked, now enthused about a possible sale.

"Black lace. I'd like a shoulder-length strap made of thick chain."

The saleswoman tried to hide her shock. Every handle in the store was either made of plastic or ribbon.

"I'm sure we can find that somewhere," she said, determined.

I was holding a crimson messenger bag. The cheapest purse was ninety-five dollars. And that was the size of a cosmetic bag.

"This is to die for. Pick one out, Raven."

I was in an awkward position. I knew my mom would freak if I let someone outside my family buy me an expensive gift. Even my mom, who wore fashionable designer purses, got them at the outlet mall.

"My treat." Mrs. Sterling's voice was intense but loving.

"That's okay. I don't need one."

The saleswoman, sniffing another sale, examined me.

There were pinks and greens and plaids. Nothing screamed my name.

"I'm not sure those prints are her style," she said to Mrs. Sterling. "We could make a black one with a red reversible. Or I do remember a special pattern—left over from Halloween."

She quickly popped in the back and returned with a wad of fabric. It was black with tiny metallic silver bats.

I couldn't help but show my infatuation for the small piece of cotton.

"To die for!" Mrs. Sterling said. "We'll take it."

My mom would kill me if she knew Mrs. Sterling bought me a hundred-dollar purse. But I was stuck in between a vampire and an overly eager shopkeeper.

"Pick out your style of purse," the woman encouraged.

"I really don't—," I tried.

"She keeps clutching the messenger bag. That will be stunning with the bat print," Mrs. Sterling said to the owner.

As the woman rang up our purchases, I could see how Mrs. Sterling transformed the shopkeeper's attitude. Either way, Mrs. Sterling wasn't affected.

I admired Alexander's mom. I never really had anyone to look up to. A role model. Of course, I had my mother and Aunt Libby. Two women who were confident and opinionated and comfortable in their own skin. But no one like me in style and taste—not until I'd met Mrs. Sterling.

* * *

Shirley's Bakery was a quaint establishment selling the freshest cookies, cakes, and donuts in Dullsville. On one side of the store a customer could buy a chocolate-covered pretzel, and on the other side was a pink-and-black-tiled ice-cream parlor.

Shirley still dished out the ice cream with her teen workers. On a clear night, the line went around the block, like for a first-run *Star Wars* flick.

Once inside, Mrs. Sterling held her umbrella proudly. She was tall and imposing, and I imagined that if anyone confronted her, though she'd behave like a lady, she'd be able to squash them like a bug.

"Two chocolate cones and one pistachio," she ordered. "Jameson's favorite," she whispered to me.

My heart melted at her kindness to her butler.

"You must be from out of town," Shirley said.

"Does it show?" she asked with a laugh. "Yes. But now we live up on Benson Hill. And your ice cream comes highly recommended."

"Why, thank you," Shirley said. "For that I'll give you an extra scoop."

We scooted back into the Mercedes. And the two of us sat, parked outside, eating our ice cream.

"I love to people watch," she said with her lyrical voice.

It wasn't something I'd ever really done. Just watch people. I'd always sensed I was the one being watched. And I never felt comfortable hanging out on the square. I preferred the park, where there was less traffic.

"Look at those two. It seems like it's their first date. How adorable," Mrs. Sterling said. "And that young man pushing a stroller while his wife and child eat their treats— it's like a greeting card." Then she spied a trio of identical tween girls sitting on a bench sharing a sundae. "Perfectly charming!"

I didn't spend much time admiring fellow Dullsvillians. But Mrs. Sterling was fascinated with them. She showed me how interesting ordinary people could be if only I'd take the time to look.

When I finally got home, I was exhilarated—like a groupie who had just met her idol.

Mrs. Sterling was beautiful, a vampire, and as confident as a queen. She was everything I wanted to be.

14

Mini-Mansion

As usual, I was unable to focus on my homework—and this time it was for a good reason. I'd finally met Alexander's parents and had a girls' night with his mother.

Still, I couldn't help but wonder what this meant for Alexander. He had been the master of the castle for months, so I imagined it was a hard transition for him now that they were occupying "his" space. I was sure that's why he'd been so grumpy at the beginning of our last date. I lay on my bean bag and wondered how my life would be if Sarah and Paul Madison lived in Europe like the Sterlings and I had full run of our home.

I'd do a total makeover of the entire Madison house. All white walls would be painted black. Bright floral curtains would be changed to dusty velvet ones. I'd remove the catalog-ordered furniture and replace it with antique thrift-store finds. I'd live by candlelight but keep the electricity for much-needed necessities, such as a refrigerator, cable TV, and my hair dryer. Alexander's coffin would be next to my bed. I'd have a huge security officer by my door so my brother wouldn't be aware of Alexander's identity. We'd stay up all night watching *The Lost Boys* and pigging out on popcorn. Billy and Henry would inhabit the basement, under my strict curfew, and fire confetti-filled missiles at Trevor's house when I commanded.

I'd exist on Count Chocula and caramel coffee lattes. School would be an optional part of the day.

My fantasy, however, was a far cry from my current living situation. I would never see such independence until I was an adult. And though I craved it and wanted to spread my bat wings without boundaries, my conservative and governing parents were crucial to my existence. I didn't have enough money for my own apartment—or the wherewithal to shop for groceries or make my own dental appointments. And when I was really down about life and love, even though I barked at their sentiments, they were my safety net. If my parents weren't around for guidance and support, my world would be darker than it already was.

Dullsville's rail yard was built in the late nineteenth century. What once must have been a thriving and highly active station, importing and exporting coal, wheat, and corn, was now a graveyard. The rail cars looked like tombstones, marking a life that once was.

Planks from tracks were missing, and it was a mystery

where some of the rail lines even led. Overgrown grass and weeds covered the rest.

Alexander asked me to meet him by the rail yard office tower. I found him leaning against a graffiti-laden boxcar whose door had probably been missing for years.

"Finally we are together," I said, squeezing him with all my might. Alexander hugged me, but he seemed distracted. "What's wrong?"

"My coffin is so empty now." His words hit me hard as I nestled into his chest.

"You resent your parents for intruding on our space. That's normal. My parents totally get on my nerves. You've been lucky. You had a vacation from them for months."

"It's more than that. But I'd rather focus on you."

I leaned my head back, exposing my bare neck. "Please, just do it now. Take me away from all this—"

"You are so dramatic. Besides, we aren't on sacred ground."

"Is that why you brought me here instead of the cemetery? So I wouldn't be tempted?"

"So *I* wouldn't be . . ."

The normal world would perceive me to be in the hands of a monster, but I knew I was in the company of a dark angel. Alexander grazed his fangs over my neck, sending me into wild giggles. Then he pulled away.

"You don't know what our lives would be like. You constantly needing me."

"But I already do."

"Believe me, Raven, I think about what it would be

like. I imagine it every day."

"What do you imagine?"

"We'd sleep in my coffin together. We'd live in the Mansion—so you could see your family—but we'd travel the world together. Rome, Paris, Greece. I'd paint pictures of you and we'd sell them in galleries across the world."

"Wow." I didn't have a clue that Alexander fantasized like I did. "Then could we? Make it everlasting?"

Just then we heard a dog bark.

"We'd better climb inside before someone spots us."

Alexander took my hand and lifted me into the rail car. I was the equivalent of a princess on a white horse being escorted by her handsome prince across a field of tulips. Except in my case everything was black and some of the flowers were dead.

I stepped into a dream world. Votives and candelabras lit the car. Crystal vases bloomed lifeless roses, and petals covered the wooden floors. The pictures of Dullsville and me that once hung on the Mansion walls were now fixed on the steel walls of the railroad car. The fragrant scent of lavender filled the air.

"I figured if I couldn't bring you to the Mansion, I'd bring the Mansion to you."

I stood frozen. My eyes began to well. Alexander's chocolate eyes gazed down at me, and his smile lit up his handsome, pale face as he waited for my response.

"I can't believe this!" I exclaimed as I examined each detail he had re-created. "This is the best present ever!"

I squeezed him so tight I thought I might pass out.

Alexander tickled my waist. His voice was soft and his lips tender. My heart filled with so much passion I thought it would burst. I wove my fingers through the length of his silky hair. We spun around, our bodies entwined, until we both became so dizzy we fell over onto makeshift throw pillows.

I didn't need a Mansion. I only needed Alexander.

The following day, I was in the garage putting air into my bike tires. My mom pulled into the drive, popped out of her car, and charged toward me.

"I've invited the Sterlings over for dinner," she declared.

"You did what?" I asked, releasing the air hose from the tire valve.

"I invited them over," she repeated.

"Why? How?" I stood up, shocked by my mother's news.

"I called them up. Why is that so strange? People have been doing that for years."

"But—"

"Mrs. Sterling was so delighted," my mom continued. "I don't think anyone in town has invited them out socially, so I was proud to be the first one."

"That is very nice of you . . . but—"

"You don't want us to meet them? Or is it that you don't want *them* to meet *us*?"

"Both."

"So you want them all to yourself." My mom sighed.

"Is there anything wrong with that? I just met them. Let me have some time alone before you start parading them through the country club functions."

"Well, if I'd known you'd felt so strongly . . . I guess I can call and cancel."

"Don't you dare! You can't; that would be rude."

"I knew you'd see it my way," she said, and gave me an overzealous mother-triumphs-again hug.

Since I was a kid, all Madison family meals were spent at the dinette—a small, rectangular wooden table with matching chairs. A few scratches and stains showed its age, like rings around a tree. Breakfast, lunch, and dinner; homework; and many school projects took place on this table and chairs. The dining room, however, was reserved for holiday and extended family meals. Suddenly, fancy tablecloths, sterling-silver candle holders, crystal salt and pepper shakers, linen napkins, and china flew out of the china cabinet.

"We don't have any black lace tablecloths," I called to my mom, who was in the kitchen preparing dinner. I searched through the cabinet drawers for Sterling-like decor. All I found in our possession was a pale crimson, a white lace, and a plastic floral one.

"Why would you want a black tablecloth?"

"Do you even know who you are inviting over?"

I settled for a brown cloth with embroidered leaves and began setting out my grandmother's china.

"I can't remember a time when you set the table without being asked," my mom said, holding a glass vase with fresh flowers. "I'll have to invite the Sterlings over more often."

I positioned six plates evenly, measuring their distance by the width of my hand.

"You don't want to set it too early. It might collect dust," she advised.

"I want to make sure it's perfect."

Henry and Billy Boy ran up from the basement like an incoming army. "When's dinner?" Billy asked.

I was aghast. "He's not going to be here, is he?"

"Of course; he's part of the family."

"But I only set six."

"Then set eight. We have twelve place settings."

I imagined the conversation switching from talk of life in Romania to talk of *Star Trek* conventions.

Rage raced through my blood. Billy Boy knew it, too. He raised his eyebrows in victory, and he and Henry took off for his room.

I followed the nerd-mates upstairs. I found my new Purse Party messenger bag on my nightstand and knocked on his door.

"No ghouls allowed," he hollered to a few boyish giggles.

I pushed the door ajar. I opened my wallet and flashed

him a five-dollar bill. "You'll ask to eat at Henry's?"

His face lit up as if I'd just shown him a mint condition Luke Skywalker action figure. "Sure."

"You promise?"

"Cross my heart."

I gave my brother the bill.

He held it tightly in his hand. "That was to ask," he said. "Not to actually stay."

My instinct was to hit him over the head with my purse. However, he had been trained by the best, so I refrained.

I dug back into my wallet. I had three singles left. "This is 'to stay,'" I said, handing him a single. "This is 'to eat.'" I handed him another bill. "And this is to 'not come back until late.'"

"We'll need money for a movie, then."

"And nachos," Henry added. "I always eat nachos at the movies."

"I bet you do. Would you like money for video games, too?"

They both nodded eagerly.

"That was a rhetorical question." I snarled. "This is all I have." I handed him a wadded ten and twenty and lint-filled change. "But you can have my firstborn if you spend the night."

"That I'll pass on," he said as I blasted out the door.

"I thought we were going to have steaks!" I said when I returned to the kitchen. I was missing the aroma of marinade and instead saw scentless water boiling on the stove.

"I decided to make pasta instead," my mom said.

"The Sterlings can't eat that. They have to eat meat. And they like it rare."

"Why—are they animals?"

I bit my black lip.

"Are you sure we can't still get a catering company?" I asked. "Or at least help in serving? They're used to having a butler."

"We are who we are—we don't change for other people. You know that. I think cheese tortellini with salad will be great. Besides, your dad is trying to cut back."

"This isn't about Dad. We are hosts."

"I'm sure they love Italian."

I imagined a bloodthirsty and starving-to-the-bone Sterling family leering at my parents for their real meal.

"Doesn't anyone in this family listen to me?" I stormed around the kitchen and opened the fridge. I didn't expect to see blood-filled smoothies, but a girl can always hope. "They don't like garlic, remember. No garlic bread."

"I know, you've told me a thousand times."

"Well, you didn't remember I requested steaks," I mumbled.

"I'll need your help with the brownies," my mom nudged.

Jameson served flaming pudding. Sarah Madison served microwave brownies.

I zapped the dessert and realized I'd spent so much time figuring out what to wear to the Sterlings', I hadn't even begun to pick out what I'd wear tonight.

I raced upstairs and obsessed about what was the perfect attire to wear as one of the Sterlings' dinner hosts. I changed outfits at least five times and, naturally, I settled on the first outfit I originally had on—a frilly black lace skirt, white bodice, black-and-red-striped stockings, and Mary Janes.

I was exhausted by the time the doorbell finally rang.

I grabbed a knitted blanket and a pair of Billy's sneakers that were sitting on the stairs and threw them into the hall closet. I straightened my skirt. "They're here!"

"Then answer the door!" my mom called.

I checked myself in the hallway mirror. I was pleased with my reflection. *Oh my!* I thought. *Reflection!* I immediately unhooked the mirror and carefully placed it in the closet.

The doorbell rang again.

"Answer the door, Raven," my mother called. "They'll think we're not home!"

I smoothed out my skirt again and opened the door. Alexander looked gorgeous in a gray silk shirt and black jeans. Mrs. Sterling was packed into a tight black dress and dark knee-high boots, and she held a black lace parasol. Her attire was a fabulous combination of sixties and goth.

Mr. Sterling sported an impressive silk suit, lavender tie, and brooding half cape.

"Welcome to our home," I said.

My mom rushed over to us, wiping her hands off with a kitchen towel.

My dad came over and did his best to conceal his shock.

Mrs. Sterling collapsed her umbrella.

"Mom, Dad, this is Mr. and Mrs. Sterling."

My mom extended her hand. "It's lovely to meet you both."

"Hello. I'm Cassandra," Alexander's mom said.

"I'm Paul, and this is Sarah," my dad responded.

"Constantine Sterling. Nice to meet you," Alexander's dad said.

"Here, let me take that," my dad said, taking the umbrella. "I didn't know it was raining."

"It isn't," she said evenly. Her violet eyelashes sparkled.

"Well, I guess you are prepared when it does."

"Come in and make yourselves at home. I'm just finishing up." My mom darted into the kitchen.

My father stuck the umbrella in the closet. "What's this doing in here?" he muttered, noticing the hall mirror lying against his tennis racket.

Dinner at the Madisons' might have been the Sterlings' first time slumming it. Our house was nice, but it wasn't a monster-size megamansion.

My father led us into the living room.

"Your house is gorgeous," Mrs. Sterling remarked.

I clutched Alexander's hand for security. Now I could see why he had waited to introduce me to his family. The pressure was enormous. What would my mother say? What did they really think of my house?

Our house wasn't tidy, but my mom did clean it. At least the sight of a few cobwebs would make them feel comfortable.

"Can I get you something to drink?" I asked. "Dinner's almost ready."

"Raven, I need you," I heard my mother bellow.

Of course she did. Now that I had company my mom was getting all demanding. I wanted to keep my eyes and ears on my father and our guests. How could I edit embarrassing conversation if I was out of earshot?

"Can I be of any assistance?" Mrs. Sterling kindly offered.

The Sterlings were aristocrats. I couldn't imagine Mrs. Sterling serving her own food. Her fingernails were so long, I wouldn't want them to break off carrying salad bowls.

"That's all right. What would you like to drink?" I asked.

"I am so bloody thirsty," Mrs. Sterling said, "I could drink a horse."

My dad laughed. "I like your sense of humor."

"How about water?" Alexander answered.

"Perfect," I said, and exited before they could change his mind. In the kitchen I tried to pick up on their conversation. I was moving quickly and the ice dropped out of my hand. I returned with three waters. The drinks shook as I brought them out on a tray.

As soon as I entered the living room, the drinks clanking together, my dad and Alexander jumped up to assist me. "I'm not sure you have a future in the restaurant biz," my dad joked.

"I see Raven as the owner of a fashionable boutique," Mrs. Sterling said.

"Really?" my dad asked. "I was hoping she'd be a tennis pro, but as you see, she doesn't like to wear white."

Great. This whole evening was going to be my dad's chance at his comedy act—with me as the source of his material.

"Dad's embarrassing me already," I said to my mom, back in the kitchen.

"He's just having fun. Maybe he's a bit nervous. The Sterlings are very interesting people."

I placed the rolls, butter, pasta, sauce, and salad on the table in record time.

"Dinner's on," my mom hollered as if she were Mrs. Walton ringing a dinner bell.

Alexander and I sat on one side and the Sterlings on the other, while my parents were at the head of the table. Our dining-room table was a third of the size of Alexander's. We all were in arm's reach of one another.

I noticed my mom staring at the wounds on Mrs. Sterling's neck. Mrs. Sterling must have sensed it, too, as she turned to my mom.

"Just a small bite I received last night. Don't worry—it's not contagious."

"I didn't mean to—," my mom said apologetically.

"I thought it was a tattoo," my dad said, and we all laughed.

I caught my reflection in the glass curio cabinet. I couldn't help notice the lack of our company's shadows.

I knew my parents were now distracted with conversation, but once the wine flowed and the carb coma hit—it might be more obvious.

"Excuse me," I said.

I dimmed the lights so the glare wasn't so noticeable.

"Good idea. This is much cozier," my mom complimented me.

"I hope pasta is okay," I whispered to Alexander.

"This dinner looks delicious," Mrs. Sterling said.

"Thank you," my mom replied. "I bet you are glad to be settled here."

"Well, we will be off again soon," Mrs. Sterling said.

"Really?" my dad said curiously. "You travel a lot."

"We're going back to Romania," Alexander's dad stated.

"So soon? You just got here," my mom noted.

"For business or pleasure?" my father wondered.

"Both," Mr. Sterling answered.

"Alexander has told us that you are an art dealer," my dad said. "What is your specialty?"

"Whatever sells."

We all laughed at his honesty.

"I have several galleries and showcase up-and-coming artists as well as the masters," he explained.

"Our country club is having an auction next month," my mom chimed in. "Mrs. Mitchell is organizing it. Have you met her?"

Alexander's parents shook their heads.

"They're auctioning paintings from professional artists," my dad said. "I'm sure you might find some wonderful additions to your collection."

"I don't think you'd find a Picasso in this town. Unless, of course, Alexander was selling his work," I said proudly.

"I'm sure you could fill several galleries with Alexander's art," my mom said. "We haven't seen his paintings yet, but Raven has told us he is quite talented."

"I thought he'd need schooling, but he has refused," Mr. Sterling said.

"He's a natural, then," my dad concluded. "My sister, Raven's aunt Libby, saw one of his paintings when Raven visited her. Libby said that Alexander's technique was extraordinary. She should know. She's in the arts."

"Well, he must take after my mother. She was very talented," Mr. Sterling said.

Alexander seemed uncomfortable. It appeared to me that Mr. Sterling didn't think Alexander was serious about his art.

"So Cassandra, what did you do today?" my mom asked.

"We mostly slept. And you?"

"I love days like those," my mom admitted. "I bet you

are still adjusting to jet lag. Sometimes that can take awhile to shake off."

"I must say that Alexander has been such a changed young man since meeting Raven," his mother said.

"That is wonderful to hear," my mom said, touched. "Alexander is so mature for his age. And always a true gentleman."

"Thank you," Mrs. Sterling responded, upbeat. "Yes, Alexander is an old soul."

"You sure raised him right," my mom continued. "Whatever you've been feeding him all these years, I think some other mothers should follow your lead."

I nudged Alexander underneath the table.

"I do keep him on a strict diet," Mrs. Sterling said in between sips of wine.

"So Constantine, do you play golf or tennis?" my dad interjected.

I thought I was going to die. But then again, Alice Cooper was an amateur golfer.

"I haven't played in years."

"So what do you do to unwind?"

"Fly."

"You are a pilot?"

"No, I—"

"My dad likes to travel," I jumped to say.

"We are hoping to take a vacation soon. It's just one day flows into another and then soon the kids are grown and the last trip we've taken was to Disney," my dad said.

"Raven tells us you like vampires?" Mrs. Sterling said directly to my father.

"We used to watch monster movies when she was a kid. I hope it didn't scar her."

"Raven's obsessed with them, if you haven't noticed," my mom teased.

"I think we have," Alexander's mom said. "It's something we share."

"You should come to Romania," Mr. Sterling suggested. "You could tour Dracula's castle."

"That sounds like a fun and very different family vacation," my dad said.

"Thank you again for inviting us, Mrs. Madison. You are a wonderful cook," Alexander blurted.

"We have plenty more pasta," my mother encouraged.

"I'm stuffed," Mr. Sterling said.

"Yes, me, too," Mrs. Sterling agreed.

"Would you like a cigar?" my dad asked Mr. Sterling.

I hated when my dad smoked cigars—though he rarely did. It smelled good for about five seconds until I began wearing it on my clothes and hair. My mother despised it as much as I did, which is odd since they spent most of their college years smoking things with all sorts of bad smells. I shooed them out to the patio as my mom and Mrs. Sterling disappeared into the kitchen.

"They seem to be hitting it off," I said to Alexander.

"This really was nice for them; they needed to get out. I think they were feeling isolated in the Mansion. Maybe if they made more friends they wouldn't want to . . ."

Alexander trailed off.

"What?"

We heard a dish break in the kitchen.

"I am so sorry," my mom said.

"No—it was me," Mrs. Sterling said as we joined them in the kitchen. A china plate was broken on the floor. "We were talking about Romania and I just asked Sarah if she believed in vampires."

"I think it's time that we were going, Mom," Alexander said.

"What's all the commotion?" my dad asked as he came in.

"Nothing. A dish just slipped through my fingers," my mom explained, discarding the broken dinnerware into the trash.

"I'd like to pay for that," Mrs. Sterling offered.

"Yes, we'll buy you a new set," Mr. Sterling said. "We insist."

"Please, it's no trouble," my mom stated with a laugh. "It gives me an excuse to go shopping."

"I had a wonderful time, Sarah," Mrs. Sterling said. "I hope we can see each other again."

"You don't have to leave yet." My mom's voice was sad, as if she was not ready for her party to end.

"Constantine, we must be going," Alexander's mother said. "We've kept the Madisons up far too long."

"We stay up late, too," my mom tried to assure her.

They stay up until at least six, I wanted to say.

"We'll have to get together again. Next time at our

home," Mrs. Sterling stated.

My parents were thrilled.

"Then it's a date. This Saturday we'll have a cocktail party. Just the four of us," said Mrs. Sterling.

"You aren't inviting us?" Alexander asked. "I think we should be there, too."

"For cocktails?" Mrs. Sterling wondered.

"And Cokes," Alexander suggested.

"Well . . . of course, darling. We'd never leave you out."

"What can we bring?" my mother asked.

Mrs. Sterling leaned in and said, "Your appetite."

The next night, Alexander and I met at his grandmother's monument in the cemetery.

"I think it went well," I said, rushing toward him.

He greeted me with a long kiss. "That was so nice of your parents to invite us. No one in town has reached out to them. It meant a lot."

"My parents really like you. And your family."

Alexander brushed my hair away from my face with his fingers. "But there are things you must know."

"Our dads got along," I said, dreaming.

"Constantine's really great. But he doesn't see me as a real artist. He thinks I'm just going through a phase."

"Why do you call him by his first name?"

"I just rarely see him. And when I do, he's always focused on his work. *Dad* never really fell off my tongue. Raven, I have to tell you something. Why I didn't introduce you to them before . . . It's why I've been distracted." Alexander paused, trying to find the right words.

"They like me, but they don't want me to become your grandmother—an outsider in her own family," I said.

Alexander nodded.

"I can imagine if my parents knew you were a vampire, they might have problems with it. I understand your parents might feel the same way about me being a mortal."

"Well, there is that . . ."

"But we all get along. Like one big extended happy family. It's just funny. If my parents knew about your parents—and you for that matter . . ."

"What do you think they'd do?" Alexander asked, pulling me toward him.

"Not let me meet you in a cemetery, on sacred ground. That's for sure."

Dullsville's cemetery was decorated for a wedding. I stood at its entrance wearing a strapless white wedding dress and long white fingerless gloves. My train was as long as a coffin. Chairs, filled with unfamiliar faces, lined the soggy grass.

Mr. and Mrs. Sterling were awaiting me underneath the wrought-iron arch. Becky was standing up there in a pink ill-fitting bridesmaid's dress. Jameson, in his chauffeur's uniform, was standing as a best man. The officiator was cloaked in a grim reaper outfit.

Alexander, beaming in a vintage tuxedo, was waiting for me.

My dad joined my side and held a tight grip on my

elbow. For some reason, I felt resistant to go—just as I had as a kid when it came time for swimming lessons. The water was always too cold, and my suit was always still damp from the day before. My dad held on tightly. "It's time to swim," he said with a wink.

We walked through the cemetery between the tombstones as raindrops hit my veil.

I tried to find my mother. She was sitting in the front row with her back toward me. When I reached her row, I heard her mumble, "Why did you want to be like her when you could have been like me."

I was appalled by her comment, but my dad still guided me to the altar.

The grim reaper's face was hidden, but Alexander was gorgeous. He took my hand and squeezed it tightly. Becky lifted my veil. My handsome vampire leaned me back and grinned. His fangs flashed. For some reason I wasn't frightened. Two stabs gently pierced the soft flesh of my neck. I became dizzy.

I could smell blood—my own—as it dripped down my neck. It drizzled down the white dress and splattered like paint.

The guests began to clap and cheer in a contagious frenzy. They rose to their feet and smiled. All of them were vampires. Even my best friend, Becky, flashed tiny fangs at me. My father grinned and my mother sneered, both bearing pearly white fangs.

"The Sterlings have come to town!" the guests cheered.

I froze, staring at my parents. This isn't what they had wanted for me—much less for themselves. And it was now too late, for all of us.

I awoke to glares from my classmates. I must have dozed off in English class. Mrs. Naper was tapping her pointer on her desk. "That makes the third time this week, Raven. I'll have to talk to your parents about your sleeping habits."

Trevor glanced back from the front row. He gave me a sexy grin and shook his head. For the first time, I was happy to see him. It was less disturbing to see my nemesis as a nightmare of my reality than to see my parents as vampires in a dream.

18

Cocktail Party

A few hours before our cocktail party at the Sterlings', I found my mom tossing dresses on her bed. She was as anxious as I had been when I was first invited to the Mansion.

"What do I wear?" she asked.

"Whatever you want."

Since my mother wasn't going to paint her nails black and wear a corset over the top of a camisole, I didn't think it really mattered what her attire was. However, she didn't feel the same.

"Should I wear this—or this?" she asked, holding up the same blouse, one in white, and one in red. "Mrs. Sterling is so stylish. Not that it's my style, but nevertheless it's bold. I don't want to offend her by appearing too conservative."

"Are you kidding?" All of a sudden my mother cared

about what the neighbors thought?

I think she was as taken by Mrs. Sterling as I was—just for different reasons. I wanted to be like Cassandra, a beautiful royal-blooded vampiress with a gorgeous vampire family, residing in an eerie mansion. But to my mom, Cassandra was exotic, unique, and worldly. Different, like my mom had been in her pre-corporate days.

"Mom, you are fine just the way you are."

"You're only saying that because you want me to hurry up."

"No, I mean it. I don't think eyebrow piercings and spider tatts will go with your Donna Karan blouses."

"You're right. I'll just be me—plain old boring me," my mother said, folding her arms.

"You are far from boring."

"I guess I just wanted you to think your mom was cool."

"You're not supposed to be cool to me. You're my mom. Do you think Grandma is cool?"

"I see your point. I didn't do too bad a job raising you after all, did I?"

"Well, if you must know, you could raise my allowance."

It was a moment I was excited about and dreaded at the same time. My parents visiting the Mansion. What would they say? What would they do? How would they respond to bloodred smoothies?

My dad inched his SUV up the Mansion's drive. Fog

hovered over the bushes and candles flickered inside the Mansion.

"It looks haunted," my mom mumbled to my father. "I know why you like coming here," she said to me. "It's very . . . mysterious."

"I'm anxious to see what it looks like inside. I feel very privileged. Like Charlie getting a chance to see the inside of the chocolate factory," my dad said.

"Promise me you both will behave. They have very different tastes. Please don't say anything rude," I said.

I walked up the uneven cracked front steps, my parents following close behind.

I knocked on the serpent knocker.

"That is quite . . . unusual," my mom remarked.

"Shhh!" I said. "You promised."

The oak door squeaked open and Jameson appeared in the entrance.

"Welcome, Miss Raven, and Mr. and Mrs. Madison. Shall I take your things?"

My mom immediately felt the chill in the air.

"Thank you, Jameson, but I'll keep my sweater." She had it tied around her shoulders but loosened it and put it back on.

"The Sterlings will be down shortly. May I get you a drink while you wait?"

"No thank you," my mother said. "We can wait for the Sterlings."

"Why don't you have a seat in the parlor room? They will only be a moment." Jameson showed us in.

Candelabras and votives filled the Mansion. Skeleton lights were strung from the ceiling. Harpsichord music played loudly. This time I expected to see a *Phantom of the Opera*–type musician banging out his melodies on a giant organ, but I found neither.

My father scanned the dusty books, and my mom fascinated herself with the vintage furniture.

"This is the home you've always wanted to live in," she said to me. "This must be a dream come true for you."

I appreciated my mother's moment of understanding.

I had a feeling that everything would be okay, though there was a teensy-weensy bit of my overactive imagination that wondered if my parents would be safe partying with two vampires on their home soil.

But when I saw Alexander enter the parlor, I knew that if there was a turn for the worse, he'd protect us from any harm.

My handsome Knight of Night came over to me and kissed me softly on the cheek. He shook my father's hand, and my mother gave him a gentle hug. He returned to me and took my hand. His hand felt strong in mine, and I squeezed it hard.

"I'm sorry to have kept you waiting. May I get you something to drink?"

"No, we were just browsing. This room is charming. I can feel the history in its walls," my mom said.

"Yes, my grandmother was very proud of this mansion. That is why I'm so horrified . . ."

We all glanced at Alexander.

". . . that some of the boards need repairing."

Alexander's comment was odd. The whole house appeared to need repairing—well beyond a few floorboards.

We heard the lyrical Romanian accents of the Sterlings as they entered.

"My apologies for our delay," Mrs. Sterling said, extending her hand to my mom, then my dad. She wore a lavender scarf around her neck. "I hope you haven't been waiting long."

"We just got here," my mom said. "The house is . . . beautiful."

"We were hoping you'd be longer so we could peek around the house," my dad blurted out.

"A tour?" Mr. Sterling asked. "I think that can be arranged. Where shall we start?"

"You'll forgive us if anything is out of order. We haven't totally settled in since we've been back," Mrs. Sterling said.

The house wasn't messy at all; in fact, everything was in its place. If anything, it was bare. Only what was needed was shown or on display. Now, dust and spiderwebs, that was a different story. There was a high volume of both.

"You've already seen Constantine's favorite room," Mrs. Sterling said, gesturing back to the parlor as we continued on. "Did Jameson tell you? When someone passed away in the family the parlor was used to view the dead."

My dad was impressed. My mom was aghast.

"Fortunately, that doesn't happen very often in our

family," she added cryptically.

"Who are the people in the hallway?" my dad asked.

"I didn't see any people," Mr. Sterling said. "Are you referring to ghosts?"

"No," my dad said with a chuckle. "Lining the hall-way."

We followed Mr. Sterling in the corridor. "These are portraits of our family."

"If you don't mind my saying . . . this guy bears a resemblance to Dracula."

"Dad!"

"No—I like your eye, Paul. We think so, too. The artist was watching too many Bela Lugosi movies when they sat down for that one."

"Alexander, would you mind going upstairs and taking over the tour? I hope I'm not being rude—I'd just like to make sure everything is in order," Mrs. Sterling said.

Order? What did that mean? What was Mrs. Sterling planning on serving us?

We followed Alexander up the red velvet stairs. The corridor was long, cold, and devoid of modern material possessions. "This is the library and these are bedrooms," Alexander explained.

My dad poked his head into the library while my mom checked out the bathroom. Antique fixtures adorned the massive room. I noticed her trying to find something.

"This is a quick tour," I said. "We're not moving in."

"I wanted to check my lipstick," she said. "But there's no mirror."

"Your makeup is fine."

"Wow—there are a lot of bedrooms," my dad said as he poked his head in each one.

"This is Jameson's room," Alexander said, showing us the butler's quarters, with its single bed and dresser. "And this is my parents'."

Mr. and Mrs. Sterling's door was slightly ajar. We could see a vanity dresser topped with assorted makeup and with a frame attached, missing its mirror. My mom peered in, brushing against the door. It opened to reveal the side of a coffin.

My mom gasped.

"What's wrong?" my dad asked, standing behind me.

My mother turned ghost white. "Nothing. I just thought I saw something, that's all. It must have been the lighting."

Alexander shut his parents' door. "I forgot. Jameson didn't get to clean it and if it isn't perfect . . ."

"We understand. I wouldn't want to give a tour of our house anytime soon," I said.

"Those stairs lead to my attic room, but I wasn't expecting—"

"I think we should help your mother," my mom said hurriedly.

Alexander and my dad talked about the Mansion as my mother pulled me to the side. "I saw a coffin in the bedroom."

"Mom. Do you really believe Mr. or Mrs. Sterling would sleep in a coffin?"

She paused. Then she let out a laugh.

"I'm sorry, Raven. This house is kind of spooky. I guess I just got caught up in it. You're right. It must have been a chest of some sort."

"Duh! You think I'd date someone whose mother slept in a coffin?"

"Well . . . ," she said, with another laugh.

"Let's hurry up before they think we're snooping," I said.

We found Mr. and Mrs. Sterling setting out napkins on the coffee table in the living room.

"Your home is very . . . historic," my mother said.

"I was hoping you'd like it," Mrs. Sterling said, pleased. "It's not everyone's taste, we know. We love it because it has character."

Just then something flew overhead. My mom let out a scream.

"Sarah! Calm down," my dad said.

"I thought I just saw a bird."

"Not a bird, Sarah," Mr. Sterling said. "It was a bat."

"A bat?"

"We are so sorry. That happens from time to time, this house being so old and all."

"Jameson!" Mrs. Sterling called.

"Can we take it home?" I asked.

"Of course not!" my mom exclaimed.

Alexander was growing paler by the moment.

Jameson rushed in holding a broom. I found it comical watching the creepy man struggle as he chased the flying creature into another room.

"Well, that doesn't happen every day." My mom laughed.

"As a matter of fact, it does," Mr. Sterling commented.

Alexander quickly changed the subject to the weather, but when the forecast called for sunny skies, Mrs. Sterling became antsy.

"What about having a few Bloody Mary's?" she suggested.

"I'm not sure the Madisons like those, Mom," Alexander said.

"Perhaps you prefer wine?" Mr. Sterling asked.

I wanted to steer my parents away from anything red, just in case there was a mixup in the kitchen.

"My parents love beer and martinis."

"Raven, don't be rude," my mother scolded.

"Of course," Mr. Sterling said. "Jameson, two martinis."

"Make mine dry, please," my dad said.

And clear, I wanted to say. Very clear.

Jameson brought us trays of fancy finger foods. Tiny pastries and miniature sandwiches filled the pewter serving plates. I was afraid to ask what was inside, but that didn't stop my mother.

"Liver. Kidney. And—" Mrs. Sterling began before my mom cut her off.

"I'm still full from dinner," she remarked, and quickly switched to the pastries.

The pastries melted in our mouths and I craved more. I was scooping up a diamond-shaped one when my mom picked up the conversation.

"I couldn't help but notice," she said. "You don't have any mirrors. Not in the bathroom or the hallway."

"We have some in the basement," Mrs. Sterling answered truthfully. I remembered seeing them when I'd snuck in one time. "We just haven't hung them up," she continued.

"But how do you put on makeup?"

"Practice. Plus, Constantine will not hesitate to tell me if it is askew."

They all laughed.

We continued to eat and drink and converse about Romania and Dullsville.

"We really appreciate your inviting us to your home," Mrs. Sterling said. "We have kept to ourselves since we returned here. This town doesn't seem to be very inviting to outsiders."

"Well, I'm hoping to fix that before it's too late," my mom said. "We wouldn't want you to feel unwelcome."

Mr. Sterling and Mrs. Sterling glanced at each other knowingly.

"I think we'll always be outsiders," Mrs. Sterling said, "no matter where we go."

As we all said our good-byes, I glanced over at my parents hugging and shaking hands with the Sterlings. I felt higher than a soaring bat, watching a scene I'd never have imagined even in my wildest dreams.

What an evening!" I said to Alexander later that night at the rail yard. He was waiting for me in the Mansion replica boxcar.

"Did they have a good time?" my handsome boyfriend asked, fishing for reassurance.

"The best time ever. On the way home, they couldn't stop talking about 'Constantine and Cassandra.' How interesting and worldly they are. They were so happy to have finally seen the inside of the Mansion. Thank you so much for inviting my parents over—and me."

"I wasn't sure . . . with the whole bat thing happening."

"Are you kidding? They couldn't stop talking about it."

"My family adores yours," he said with a twinkle in his eye. Then he placed his hand on mine. "But you must understand, I don't want you to get too excited—"

"We all were excited. My dad was so impressed with the Mansion. It was a tour of a lifetime."

"I'm glad they liked it, but—," he started.

"These last few days were more amazing than I could have imagined," I said, cutting him off. "I love your parents. Can we trade?"

"Our parents? Sure. I think yours are cool."

"What? No way!"

"My mom carries an umbrella in the moonlight," he said with a chuckle. "And my dad insists on wearing a cape."

I had no idea Alexander viewed his parents like I viewed mine—slightly embarrassing. "I love your parents' style. My mom and dad think plaids or pinstripes is all the rage."

"Yours are way cooler!" he said, tickling my side.

"That's just because they aren't *your* parents. If you lived with them, you'd change your mind."

"And you might, too," he said. "Especially when you know that—"

"What was I thinking when I was spying on those two lovely people outside the Mansion? They don't have skeletons! Not in their closet, or otherwise."

"There's something I need to tell you." Alexander turned serious.

"I was just being immature. Please don't tell them."

"I won't."

"Promise."

I began to kiss my boyfriend, then snuggled against

his chest. "This is so much better than I imagined. I love having your parents in town. So we give up some independence. Who cares? We're gaining so much more."

"I have to tell you—"

"No—there's something I really want to tell you." I stared into his deep, dark eyes. "I finally think my life is perfect."

Alexander looked shocked, then pleased.

"So what do you want to tell me?" I asked.

"It can wait," he said resignedly.

Alexander kissed me good night with such emotion it was as if he were kissing me for the first time—or the last.

The next morning, I arose from a dead sleep and walked glass-eyed downstairs in my slippers and pajamas. I headed straight for the coffeemaker.

My parents seemed strange—odder than usual. Solemn, like someone had died. My mom was hovering over the Sunday paper on the kitchen table.

"Maybe she already knows," she said.

I poured some coffee. "Knows what?"

"It's funny. The Sterlings didn't mention anything last night. You'd think they would have."

"Maybe they are buying a new house? Something more modern? Something without bats."

"What are you talking about?" I dragged my feet and leaned on the table.

My dad pointed to the paper.

Under the real estate column was a picture of the Mansion:

For sale—Three acres.
Sterling Estate, Benson Hill.
Berkley Realtors

My heart sank to my empty stomach.
The Sterlings were selling the Mansion!
This was what Alexander had been trying to say. Why his mother and father kept saying they'd be in town for only a few months. Why Alexander had been preoccupied and in an unusually dark mood. If there wasn't a Mansion—there'd be no Alexander.

Alexander, the love of my life, was moving back to Romania.

I pedaled my bike the entire way to Dullsville's cemetery, tears streaming down my cheeks like dripping blood. Out of breath, I flung my Trek against the brick wall and scaled the fence. Votives on tombstones lit my way through the dusky graveyard.

As I ran through the graveyard, rain began to drizzle down and extinguish the votives as I passed them. Fog slowly enveloped the landscape as if it were trying to keep me away.

In the distance, Alexander was standing next to his grandmother's monument. I stormed over to him.

"I don't want you to leave!" I cried.

"What are you talking about?" he asked.

"I saw the ad in the paper! Your parents are selling the Mansion. Why didn't you tell me?"

"I wanted to, but I just needed to get some answers first."

"Answers? You are moving back to Romania! I don't want you to leave." I clutched my boyfriend for dear life.

"I know," he said, holding me tight. "I don't either—that's why I'm trying to figure out something."

"Why do you have to move back now?" I asked, staring up into his soft brown eyes. "After all we've been through? When we have finally gotten the Maxwells off yours, mine, and Dullsville's back? This is the thanks you get?"

"That's exactly why it's time for me to return home—according to my parents. By reuniting Valentine with his brother Jagger, I ended our family feud. Now my parents want me to return to Romania so we can be a family again."

"Your life is here now!"

"I know. I've tried to explain. And just as bad, they see no reason to keep the Mansion. So now I really have nowhere to go!"

"You'll stay here and live with me. My parents won't mind."

"I can't do that—then they'll know . . ."

Alexander had a point. If Alexander slept under the same roof as my parents, there would be no way to hide that he'd be sleeping during the day in a coffin.

"What are we going to do? You can't leave, Alexander. Let me talk to them. Once they see my side—"

"I'm not sure they can be convinced. I've tried everything. Yelling, sulking. I am their son. They want me with them. I can respect that. But they are ruining my life."

"And mine! They can't do this, Alexander! I love you!"

I held on to Alexander hard and sobbed uncontrollably. "I understand why they miss you—they love you as much as I do. But why can't they just live here?"

"Because their business is in Europe. And they want us to be around our kind. The reason they sent me here was because it was isolated, and it's now the reason they want me home."

"You aren't isolated anymore. You've gone to dances and dinners and dates. Can't they see how much you've thrived in such a short time?"

"I've tried to explain it to them. I'm not sure they see it, though. They're old school."

"I never realized that my biggest conflict in our relationship wouldn't be me being a mortal and you a vampire, or revenge from some bloodsucking white-haired immortal, but your sweet parents."

Alexander was silent.

"It's me—" I collapsed in front of a tombstone. "If I were like Luna, from a vampire family, then they'd approve of me."

"They adore you."

"But I'm not a vampire. Romania is half a world away. I can't live a second without you—much less an eternity!"

"I know, me neither."

"Then tell them you won't go!"

"I have."

"And what did they say?"

"That my home is in Romania."

"I'm going to talk to them," I said vehemently, rising

from the ground. "Let's go now. When they see how much my life will be destroyed without you, they might change their mind."

But Alexander didn't move. Instead he pulled me to him and held me close as I continued to sob.

"I didn't see this coming," Alexander confessed. "I knew when they were arriving here that they'd cramp our style, but never to this degree."

Then my despair turned to anger. "Why didn't you trust me with this news? I don't understand why you didn't tell me right away. I had to read about it in the paper."

"I didn't want you to hear about it at all."

And then I faced him head-on, exposing the saddest part of my soul to him. "You want to leave, don't you?"

Alexander grasped my shoulders. "Don't ever say that—not for a minute—don't you ever think that. My home is here, with you. Now and forever."

I fell into him and we held each other.

"This is why you were keeping your parents away from me?"

"I needed time."

"I can't even bear the thought," I began. "This isn't possible! We'll never see each other again. I'm not letting you go! You should have told me."

I knew Alexander's parents had missed him. Their only son, several time zones away. Left alone to be attended by a single butler. This wasn't what they wanted for him. He was supposed to be hiding from the Maxwells, not falling in love.

"I was trying to figure out a plan."

"I'm all about figuring things out. And in this case, I think I know exactly what to do."

"Yes?"

"A solution to your problems and mine."

"Okay . . ."

"We're on sacred ground."

"Yes we are."

"I'd be yours forever."

"No—that's not an option." Alexander stepped back.

"It's our only chance," I said, tugging on his shirt. "I would be just like you—and your family. Then they won't worry about you being the only vampire in town."

"It's not time—"

"Is there any other time better than this? Is there any better reason? If not now . . . then when?"

Alexander gazed down at me. His eyes were loving, yet sad. "You don't understand what you are asking me to do."

"I absolutely do. If I become a vampire, we will be bonded forever—together for eternity. If I stay a mortal, I'll never see you again."

Alexander paused. He was as dreamy as the first time I saw him. His hair blew in the breeze. "My home is here," he said, "with you the way it is now."

"You're the one making the decision for me," I challenged. "Maybe I should make it for myself."

"What would you do if it was the other way around?" he suddenly asked me. "And there was some way I could be just like you—a mortal. Then what?"

Take the vampire out of Alexander? I hesitated. I pondered the thought of changing Alexander. I never realized the strain and burden I was placing upon him to fulfill my dream. What if I changed him and he didn't like being a mortal? What if it changed his personality? What if he was bitter and unhappy and, most of all, blamed me?

I never thought of it that way.

"Do you only like me because I'm a vampire?" he asked.

"Of course not. I'd like you if you were a troll. But it is who you are. I wouldn't want to change you."

"And that is how I see you." He cupped my face in his hands. "I love you just the way you are."

"So you wouldn't like me if I were a vampire?"

"Of course I'd love you, but . . . what if you didn't like being a vampire?" Alexander asked.

"But I'd love it! I've always dreamed of being like you."

"You'd never be able to tell your family about your new identity. And if you did, do you think they'd be happy? Their daughter is a bloodsucking vampire? It might be fun in theory until you have to leave town because you are being persecuted, like my grandparents. You think you are an outsider now, but what do you think you will become as a member of the Underworld?"

I really hadn't thought of all the details, just the highlights.

"So when you say, 'Just bite me,' it is always much more complicated than that. I'd be making a decision for you—for the rest of your life. And it's not an easy decision to make."

Alexander was always looking out for me. Not just presently, but forever.

"You can't leave Dullsville. Promise me you won't!" I said.

"I promise—to the best of my ability. I'm trying to figure out a solution, every minute of every day."

He squeezed my shoulders.

"Besides," he continued, "I can't leave you here alone with Trevor Mitchell."

I thought of the Mansion, of all the time I'd spent in Alexander's coffin, the nights watching him paint or walking through the corridors by candlelight.

"My heart is breaking," I said.

"Mine is, too. It's something I never thought was a possibility. I thought the Mansion would remain our family's forever. And I'd remain in it."

"Now you'll live in Romania?" I asked. "I'll have to come with you. It's the only way I'll survive."

"We can't be so grim yet," he said softly, touching my cheek. "At this point there have been no offers on the house. There's still time to figure out a plan."

21

News Travels Fast

When I arrived home, my parents were on the edge of their couches waiting up for me. I was racked with pain and torment.

"So, what did Alexander have to say?" my mom asked. "Are they staying in town?"

I shook my head.

"You must be devastated."

"I am!"

Tears began to roll down my already-soaked cheeks.

"We were so taken with his parents, too. We were hoping to spend more time with them. I'm so sorry, honey."

I could barely speak.

"I thought they liked it here, but I must say that I can imagine it would be difficult for them," my mom said.

"Why, because she wears a corset? And uses an umbrella to block the moonlight?" I asked.

"You gripe about how conservative this town is," my mom said. "They might be seeking someplace more cosmopolitan."

"What are the chances—if Alexander does move—that I could go with him?" I asked my dad.

"Zero," he answered.

"Honey," my mom said softly, "I know he is your first love."

"He's my only love!"

"I know," she continued, "but you are only sixteen."

"I'm almost seventeen. Juliet was married at that age!"

"And look what happened to her," my dad said.

"This isn't funny! If Alexander moves, my life is over—pure and simple. I'll never wake up again." I burst into tears.

My mom hugged me like I was a child.

"Why can't the Sterlings like it here?" I sobbed. "Why do they have to go back to Romania?"

"I'm sure they have family there," my mom said, brushing my hair away from my tearstained face. "That is their home."

"But this is Alexander's home. If we buy it—then Alexander can live there. He's almost eighteen, you know."

"I'm not sure we can afford two homes."

"But can't you try? Use my college money. I'll get a job."

"Now you are thinking." My dad smiled.

"I mean it," I said. "I'll do it." But then I calculated the wages I'd made when I worked at Armstrong Travel. "It would take me years working part-time to earn enough for a house," I said, frustrated. "By then I'll be buying into a retirement community."

"When your mother went back home at the beginning of college summer break," my dad said, "I was so lonely. I wrote her letters every day and called her. That was long before the Internet and cell phones."

"An e-mail is not going to replace Alexander," I said, and stormed off to my bedroom. "Nothing will."

This was one time there was nothing my parents could say that would comfort me.

By the following day the news that the Benson Hill Mansion was for sale had swept through Dullsville like a tornado. However, the only damage it was causing was to my heart.

"What are you going to do?" Becky asked at my house the next morning as I was still lying in bed. "Is Alexander moving, too? Where is he going to live?"

"I don't know."

"Well, get up. We're going to be late. I mean, later than usual."

"I don't want him to move. I'd die."

"I don't want him to move and he's not even my boyfriend. He's so perfect for you. And I'd hate to see you without your true love."

"This is, like, the worst news ever!" I cried out. It was true—there was no way around it. My world was crashing around me. "I can't go to school today!"

Becky tugged at my shirt. "You have to go. I'm not

going to let you stay here and sulk. School will get your mind off of it."

After splashing cold water on my face and promising to help solve my problem, Becky was successful at dragging me to school. But when we arrived I was far from distracted.

"The Mansion's for sale and Alexander has to move back to Romania," Becky said as soon as she saw Matt.

"My parents told me last night when I got home. That totally sucks, Raven. Word has it that they are selling it and are going to build a house next to the cemetery," he said.

Word has it? It was just announced in the paper yesterday morning. "Who did you hear that from—Trevor?"

"How did you know?" Matt asked, like I was clairvoyant.

Even Trevor's scenario was better than the reality. At least Alexander would remain in Dullsville.

I was as miserably morbid as my black attire. I spent the day daydreaming about a life in Romania with the Sterlings. The four of us as vampires, without any downside. A life of eternal love and beauty and moonlight.

Before class I was at the vending machine buying a soda.

"Finally that horrible mansion is for sale," I overheard a Pradabee say. "Hopefully they'll burn it down and put up a shopping mall."

"So you finally scared him away," Trevor said at my locker before English class. "I guess when his parents saw you, they had to pack their coffins."

"Don't you even start with me. Not today."

"Well, when then? When will we start our essays?" he asked. "I have our list of questions and my answers are blank," I said.

"To match your brain? That's not my fault."

"Half the soccer team is almost finished with theirs and we haven't even started. I know you're a procrastinator, but I'm not cramming this in the night before it's due. Unless we pull an all-nighter—then I'm game." His suggestive gaze bore through me. "I know how you like to sleep in."

I snarled and slammed my locker shut. "I have a lot on my mind."

Trevor blocked my exit.

"You'd better do this assignment. You heard what Mrs. Naper said. If I fail this, it could affect my grades for college. I'm not going to spend the rest of my life in prison with you."

"We'll finish it in time. I've just been preoccupied."

"Doing what? Polishing gravestones? Painting your nails with blacktop? Conjuring the dead?"

Now he was getting on my bad side. "Then maybe I won't do it," I challenged him.

Trevor paused. His face grew red with anger. "I knew that was your plan all along. I'm not going to let you ruin my chances for a soccer scholarship, Monster Girl."

The bell rang, ending our hostile discussion.

"Don't bother asking me to walk you to class," he said sharply.

Here I was worried Trevor was planning to sabotage

me when all along he was thinking I was going to do the same to him. My nemesis and I were more alike than I ever would care to admit.

"Remember, I know where you live," he said in his most threatening voice, "and that monster family, too. And believe me, they will be here for a while. That house won't sell."

Trevor started off for English class in a huff.

I was taken aback by my nemesis' last statement. I raced after him.

"What do you mean the Mansion won't sell?" I asked, jumping in front of him.

"Who do they think they can sell that bat trap to?" he asked. "It's an eyesore. And my dad says it's a major money pit. With all the new houses being built, who would buy a ghost-filled broken-down home when someone could buy a brand-new one?"

Trevor's injurious comment was actually a blessing in disguise. If the Mansion didn't sell, then Alexander couldn't move. My boyfriend could remain in Dullsville forever.

"I could almost kiss you," I surprised myself by saying.

"Then why don't you?" he asked, his eyes piercing through mine.

Just then the second bell rang.

"There's not enough time!" I said, and escaped into class.

22

Rumor Starter

A Berkley Realty FOR SALE sign was stuck on the lawn of the Mansion. I wanted to rip it out of the ground and throw it over the iron gate.

I wasn't sure how I would react to Mr. and Mrs. Sterling now that I knew their true plans for Alexander and the Mansion. I dearly loved them like my own parents, but I was obviously conflicted. I knew they weren't trying to hurt me and my boyfriend, but their decision was breaking my heart.

I waited outside the Mansion's door, barely able to breathe. I knocked several times.

The door finally creaked open and Alexander appeared. "They're out," he said.

I sighed. My anxiety flew out of my body like a bat from an attic. I entered the Mansion and gave my boyfriend a big kiss.

"I wasn't sure if I was going to have to beg them on my hands and knees or just burst out in tears."

Alexander gently laughed, but it was apparent by his hollowed cheeks and bloodshot eyes that he hadn't slept.

"I have great news," I exclaimed.

"I could use some."

"I figured out the perfect solution," I said.

"You did?" Alexander perked up.

I took a breath, excited by my problem solving. "You can't move out of the Mansion if no one buys it . . ."

Alexander nodded. "True . . ."

"So . . ."

"So?"

"So, we have to make sure no one does."

"How are we going to do that?" he asked.

"Glad you asked. Gossip runs through this town like a flood. Usually the rumors are about you, your family, or me. Now we'll be the ones to spread them about ourselves."

"What will we spread? How can we convince people not to buy the Mansion?"

I hated to disappoint him. He was so proud of his grandmother's mansion. Just as I adored it, he obviously did even more.

"Have you been around this town?" I asked. "I can't imagine anyone would be interested in buying the Mansion anyway, with all the rumors surrounding it for years. But now that it's for sale, we can't take any chances. We have to spread our own. Verify the Mansion is worse than they thought. Bats, mold, or rusty pipes. None of these women would step one of their Prada-wearing feet inside even to view it."

Alexander's pale face lit up.

"But what if someone from outside of town comes to take a look."

"They have to stop at Mickey's gas station. Or stay at Dullsville's bed and breakfast. They'll find out fast enough about the money-pit mansion and then we'll be able to hear their tires screeching away."

He picked me up and kissed me for a long time.

"Where do we begin?" he asked with renewed hope.

"We'll have to set everything in motion tonight. We can't waste any time."

Alexander and I met Matt and Becky by the fountain at Dullsville's town square.

Matt was in his jersey and soccer cleats and Becky had her pink sweater tied around her waist.

"Thanks for helping us, guys," I said. "We can cover more terrain if we have more mouths."

"We'd do anything to help Alexander stay in town," Becky said.

"Now, the key spots for tonight are the square and Dullsville's country club," I told them. "I'll cover school tomorrow."

"Matt can get the two of us into the club," Becky offered. "No problem."

Sporting soccer cleats and dirt-stained elbows at the conservative club were even more favorable than a black lace bodice and combat boots.

"Meet you back here in an hour," I said.

Alexander and I took the north side of the square, while Becky and Matt took the south.

We popped in and out of boutiques fake browsing and zealously talking about the miserable condition of the Mansion. The sight of Alexander and me together on the square was enough to get gossip going, but the fact that they had inside dirt—literally—on the Mansion made every patron's and salesclerk's ears perk up.

"Mission accomplished," I said as Alexander and I headed back to the fountain.

"Hey—you got Shirley's side," Becky said, already waiting.

"We planned on that," I said, nudging her.

"My treat." Alexander spoke with the same authority as a coach buying his players food after a win.

"No one ever listens to what I say," my shy best friend said as we headed into Shirley's. "But when we brought up the Mansion and the cracks in the foundation—everyone in the restaurant heard."

"It could have been because you were almost screaming," Matt said. "And we didn't have a reservation."

Just then an elderly couple sitting at a small table sharing a sundae glared back at us.

The woman said, "I think I heard that girl say that mansion has cracks in the foundation."

"I know," the man replied. "I thought he said his girlfriend ran screaming from it."

I gave Alexander's hand an extra squeeze and the thumbs-up to Matt and Becky.

Assorted dripping ice creams in tow, Becky drove us to Dullsville's country club, which was a snobby members-only club sprawled out over several acres. It included indoor and outdoor tennis courts, an eighteen-hole golf course, a gift and pro shop, and a four-star restaurant. Signs about the upcoming Annual Art Auction lined the grass like it was election day.

"We'll wait here," I said to Matt and Becky.

For a few minutes, members with tennis rackets, golf clubs, and yoga mats were coming out of the club—returning from workouts like it was their job. When it quieted down, a couple carrying boxes filled with pottery struggled to open the front door. Alexander jumped out of the truck and opened the clubhouse door for them.

"That is as close as I could get without a white shirt," he said when he got back into the truck. We held hands with crossed fingers until Becky and Matt returned.

By the time I got home, word had traveled so quickly about the undesirable money pit on Benson Hill that my parents had already heard the news and were greatly concerned.

"Maybe you shouldn't return to the Mansion." My mother confronted me as I started for the stairs.

"Why?" I asked.

"I heard the walls could fall down at any minute."

"I thought you didn't believe in gossip. Besides, who told you that?"

"That doesn't matter," she began, then shouted, "Paul—"

"But the game's almost over—," he hollered back.

"Paul, this is important."

My dad reluctantly joined us, clutching the remote like it was a lifeline.

"It's about Raven visiting the Mansion," my mom said. "I think until Alexander moves, it is best they spend time over here."

"You can't ban me from the Mansion!" I exclaimed.

I had no idea my plan would work so well. But now it was working against me.

"That house is in dire straits," my mom went on.

"I thought it was pretty sound. It was old and dusty, but I think it was as sturdy as a castle," my dad said.

"See!" I pleaded.

"But there were bats," my mom argued. "You both saw them."

"But I love bats."

"They are flying rodents," she challenged.

"Not all of them."

My parents both looked at me curiously.

"Sarah, can we discuss this later?" my dad suggested.

"Mom, those are just rumors. You've taught me all my life not to believe the negative gossip in this town. Are you telling me, in this case, that your own advice has been wrong?"

For a moment, my dad was no longer interested in the game's outcome, only in my mother's response.

"Fine. Rumors are just that. I was inside the house, too. And it was a wonderful house."

"Thanks, Mom," I said, and took off for my room.

"But just as a precaution," she called, "maybe you and Alexander could start hanging out in his gazebo."

I had never been so eager to return to school as I was the next day.

I blabbed about Alexander's haunted, smelly, or leaking mansion (depending on my mood) in the cafeteria, gym, and hallways. The day flew by and I happily headed for sixth bell, until someone stopped me on the stairs.

"Listen, Monster Girl," Trevor said. "I should have known when I picked you as a partner that I was picking the bottom of the barrel. But even I didn't realize how deep that barrel was. Either you meet me today or I'm heading straight for Mrs. Naper."

I was grateful to Trevor. Though I'd never tell him that, I felt confident that Alexander would now remain in Dullsville. I hated to do the paper, much less see Trevor, but it was something I had to complete. And there wasn't any reason to postpone it any longer.

"Sure, today is as good as any," I said.

Trevor was surprised by my positive response. He glared at me skeptically. "I know . . . you're not going to show up."

"Why would I do that?" I asked. "That's so third grade."

I wanted to meet my nemesis at a neutral place. I didn't want him to use this as an opportunity for him and his soccer-snob posse to ambush the outsider. I needed some protection—a place I knew people would be around. The town square. The main library. The police station.

We settled for the mall food court. Dullsville Mall was probably no different from any other mall in America. It had the same dress, shoe, candle, lotion, lingerie, earring stores, and kiosks as any mall. I wasn't a mall rat but rather a thrift-store junkie. But there was one thing I couldn't resist at the mall: the food court. Every time my mom or Becky dragged me there for a day of shopping, I was like a vulture on an abandoned carcass as I sampled the Icees, pizza, or free Chinese meat on a stick.

Trevor found me waiting with a slice of cheese pizza and a frozen cherry drink at a table in the center of the food court.

"At last I have you all to myself," Trevor said.

"Evidently not." I pointed to a kid from the next table, waving to us like we were his family.

"Hello," the cute boy said. The small child reminded me of Trevor when he was in kindergarten—perfect blond hair, perfect white teeth, perfectly pressed clothes.

"Children are a great judge of character," Trevor commented.

"That's why he's waving at me, not you."

"Turn around, Lance. Sorry he was bothering you." The mother picked up her son and held him on the other side of their table.

Trevor took a bite of my pizza.

"Hey, get your own!"

"I heard about the Mansion," he said. "I told you it was an eyesore. Rotting away. I can't believe you hang out in that hellhole. But maybe that's why you call it home."

"You're right. When I was there last week, we discovered a room full of flies. Just like the Amityville Horror."

"And you think that's cool?"

"Why wouldn't I? Now, do you want to continue to talk more about how gross the Mansion is—"

"No—let's get started."

I hadn't even looked at the brief question sheet. It was folded up and stuck in my English notebook. Of course Trevor kept his pristine in a folder marked "English Lit."

"Do you want to go first?" he asked. "Or shall I?"

I didn't answer.

"Please. Let me get this over with." He took out a pen, leaned in close, and began to read. "'When you were in kindergarten, what did you want to be?'"

I glared back at him.

I remembered that first day of kindergarten as clear as if it were yesterday. I had replied, "A vampire."

"A princess," I said.

Apparently Trevor remembered my real answer, too. I guess it wasn't every day that one had a classmate as odd as I had been and still appeared to be.

"That's not what you said," he challenged. "You said, 'A vampire.'"

"Really? I don't recall. So you are going to write that down?" I asked worriedly.

I knew I was going to stand in front of my class and say, "I wanted to be a vampire." Trevor would then say, "Duh," and the classroom would fill with laughter and mocking students.

Trevor scribbled something down on the sheet.

"'When you were little, what inspired you to feel this way?'" Then he paused and asked, "Looking in the mirror and having it crack in two?"

Instead of clobbering him, I laughed—the kind of laugh that escapes into the air before you can catch it. The kind of chuckle that shows a tiny form of acceptance.

Trevor obviously didn't expect me to find his remark entertaining. He was primed for a fight. We both cracked up and locked eyes. His gaze lingered a little too long, not in a creepy way, but in a way that says *I'm not ready to let this moment go.*

I felt strangely attracted to this nemesis of mine. I hated that we had any civility between us. But mostly I hated that I'd let my guard down.

I was born that way, I wanted to say. Perhaps a psychologist might trace my wanting to be a vampire back to time spent with my father watching Dracula movies. And when my brother was born all that changed. Nosferatu kept me company on the lonely nights they were tending to the crying Nerd Boy.

"No," I finally said. "It was when I didn't see my reflection."

"Fine, I'll write that," he said. "Next question. 'Do you still have that same wish you had in kindergarten?'"

"Yes, I'm sixteen and I still want to be a vampire," I said sarcastically. I really was masking my innermost feelings. In fact, that is *exactly* what I wanted to be.

I knew what Mrs. Naper was getting at. Some people change their minds along their life's path. And some people come into this world knowing exactly what they want to do. I was in the latter group.

"'What do your parents do? Would you want to follow in their paths?'" he continued.

"What do you think?"

I took out my paper. "I bet I can answer your questions without even asking you. When you were in kindergarten you wanted to be Superman, probably because you watched it on TV and liked being a superhero. But now, you obviously don't want to run around with a pillowcase cape. You want to be a professional soccer player. But you are afraid that once you get out of this small town, where you *are* Superman, you'll find out there are better players with more speed and quicker moves. And it is that part of you that when doing an assignment like this would write 'real estate developer,' like your father. Because you are afraid of failure and you don't have the courage to write down what you really want to be."

Trevor was immobilized and turned ghost white. He was blown away, as if by knowing him all these years I'd read his soul. I wasn't sure if this realization angered him or made him more attracted to me. I wasn't going to stay to find out.

I put the sheet in my backpack and left.

I could only imagine that in the spot regarding what I wanted to be in kindergarten, he crossed out *vampire* and wrote *psychic*.

Voices from Beyond

lexander and I were in his attic room. My boyfriend was painting a beautiful picture of the rail yard while I attempted to write my English essay on my mom's laptop. But I was too distracted to begin to write about possible career choices—not only because Alexander was quite the handsome artist, glowing and focused on his creation, but because I could hear the muffled voices of Alexander's parents talking in their bedroom, one floor below.

I could barely make out a few words. *Mr. Berkley. Sale. Romania.*

"I'll be right back," I said to Alexander, but he was so engrossed in his brushstrokes that I'd probably be back before he even noticed I was gone.

I snuck down the attic stairs and tiptoed past his parents' bedroom. The door was ajar. The bathroom was only a few doors down, and if I hung out inside I'd be able to hear their voices echo off the empty walls.

"Mr. Berkley says we need to put money into renovations before this house will ever sell," I heard Mr. Sterling say as I passed their doorway. I remained by a hallway table just outside their door.

"I think it's perfect the way it is," Mrs. Sterling responded.

"I agree. I'm not changing a thing. My mother built this house the way she wanted it and it will remain that way until there is a new owner."

"Maybe it's the real estate agency we should change," Mrs. Sterling offered.

There was a slight pause.

"Constantine," Mrs. Sterling began in a soft yet concerned voice. "Perhaps we are making a mistake by putting the Mansion up for sale at all."

"I know, Cassandra. I've been wrestling with that, too. This has not been an easy decision. I've tried to explain that to Alexander. But our lives are in Europe. And now it's time for us to return. All of us. Our home has always been in Romania. We are too old to change all that now."

"I guess you are right. But I do worry—"

"I don't understand it," Mr. Sterling added, changing his tone. "Mr. Berkley said not one person has shown interest. He explained that the townspeople have told him awful things about our home. I'm not sure why anyone would say such things. No one, besides the Madisons, has been inside."

The floorboard underneath me squeaked so loudly, I

thought one would be able to hear it in Romania.

The bedroom door creaked open.

Mr. Sterling appeared, and behind him a very tall and statuesque Mrs. Sterling.

The bathroom doorway that once looked so close now seemed miles away.

"Raven," Mrs. Sterling said. "We didn't know you were here."

"I was just on my way—"

"We've been meaning to talk to you," she said, "now that you've heard about the Mansion going on the market."

I didn't move.

"I know it must be hard for you, Raven—as it is for us," Mrs. Sterling said in a soothing voice.

I nodded.

"You have done so much for Alexander," she continued. "I know it will be difficult for him being away from you. So you must promise me you'll visit."

Under normal conditions, the thought of going to Romania and seeing Alexander's family would be the thrill of a lifetime. However, if I had a choice, I'd rather vacation in Romania and visit my boyfriend on Benson Hill.

"I promise," I said in agreement.

Alexander appeared at the foot of the stairs.

"What's going on down here?"

"Nothing," Mrs. Sterling said. "We were just passing in the hall."

* * *

I felt a tinge of sorrow for the Sterlings. They were just as torn as we were about the move. They were making what they thought was the best decision, even if it wasn't the choice Alexander and I would make.

I couldn't concentrate on writing, and Alexander needed a break from painting. It was getting late, so he drove me home.

"I think our plan is working," I said as he walked me to my door. "At this rate, you'll be here longer than the Mansion has."

Alexander leaned in and gave me a blissful kiss.

For the first night in a long time, I actually got a good night's rest.

Unfortunately the next guy's face I had to see was Trevor's.

"We haven't answered everything," my nemesis said, finding me on the lawn after school.

"I think you can fill in the blanks," I replied.

"I can give you a lift home. We could do it in the car."

I glared back.

"I mean the assignment," Trevor said, raising an eyebrow.

"I'd rather walk."

"When are you going to admit that you are avoiding me because you're hot for me?"

"When hell freezes over."

"You should know about hell—you live there. How about you step up to the plate and finish the job?" Trevor challenged.

I thought for a moment. I was slightly taken with the idea of having my own goth fashion magazine like Becky and I had discussed, but I couldn't possibly share that with Trevor. I'd only be ridiculed. Instead I said, "Okay, Soccer Boy. Figure out a career for me. Something that will make me money so I can be self-reliant."

Trevor opened his notebook. I could see several typed pages of his essay were already complete.

"What's wrong with a man taking care of you?" he asked. "Someone rich. And powerful."

"I already have that," I admitted.

"And blond."

"I like dark hair."

"And popular."

He did have me on that. Neither Alexander nor I were popular. But Trevor Mitchell? He could have been voted prom king in the first grade.

"Isn't fame important to you?" he asked, inching closer. "Everyone knowing your name?"

"I think they already do."

"But not for the right reasons," he said with a chuckle.

"I'm not interested in being famous. I'm interested in being me."

Trevor shook his head and jotted a few notes down in his notebook. "So where did we leave off? Do your parents want you to follow in their footsteps?"

"No. Is this over yet?" I whined.

"What do you like to do on a rainy day?" he asked.

"Sit outside."

"What do you like to do on a sunny day?"

"Sleep."

"Do you think of yourself as creative?"

"No."

"You don't?" he asked, surprised. "With the way you dress and make yourself up? I think you've always been creative. Like a clown."

"Do you want me to take you down now? Or do it in front of the class?"

"Calm down. What is your favorite outfit?"

"Hmm. My corset prom dress."

"When you close your eyes, who do you dream about?"

"Alexander."

"If you had one guy in school to kiss, who would that be?" he asked, leaning toward me.

"This isn't on the sheet. None of these questions are, bonehead!"

With Trevor, sometimes it was difficult to keep straight who was kidding who.

"I was just making sure you were paying attention. I've finished the interview portion. Now I can just write the essay."

"So—we don't have to meet again?"

"I've finished my part," he said coyly, and gave me the completed interview sheet. "Now it's time to finish your questions about me."

Trevor's interview sheet was blank. I quickly jotted down some answers to the questions and handed it to him.

"You won't get an A for handwriting," he said.

Trevor and I rose and dusted the dirt off our jeans. "Our next date will be in front of class," he said.

I couldn't help but feel a twinge of kindness toward him, as he had inadvertently helped Alexander remain in the Mansion.

"I'm off to meet my father," he said as he got into his Camaro. "Did you hear? My dad might buy the Mansion."

I stopped dead in my tracks.

"What did you say?"

He grinned a wicked grin. "I was waiting to tell you until after I got my interview portion completed. . . . We were talking about the Mansion at dinner last night and how word around town is no one will buy it because it's a hideous money pit. My dad said that the land upon which it sits is valuable property in its own right. It will be cheaper to hire a wrecking ball and bulldozer. Just thought you'd want to know. It'll make a great strip mall."

I was floored. I had no idea my own plan would turn against me. And of course, Trevor was just the person to do it.

"No—you can't buy it!" I said, my body filled with rage. "You can't buy it—and you can't tear it down."

"I know *I* can't, Monster Girl. But my dad can."

Trevor's father owned half the town of Dullsville. I wouldn't ever want Benson Hill to fall into that half.

"I'll tell my dad to save a few bricks when he tears it down. You can have them as a souvenir. I won't charge you very much, since they're worthless," he said, and rolled up his window and sped off.

I waited impatiently outside the Mansion's gate.

"I need to speak with Alexander," I told Jameson as soon as he opened the front door.

"He's still sleeping, Miss Raven."

I guess Alexander, like me, was finally having a good night's—or in his case, day's—slumber.

"This can't wait." I spoke with authority and urgency.

"I'll see what I can do. Wait in the study."

I paced in the old, dusty, book-filled room. It was several minutes later when Alexander appeared in jeans and a T-shirt.

"What's wrong?" he asked.

"Everything!" I rushed over to him. "But we have to talk privately."

"The gazebo?" he suggested.

"No—a place where no one on earth can hear us."

Alexander parked the Mercedes in front of the cemetery's entrance. We hurried toward his grandmother's monument. The only sound we heard were a few crickets chirping.

"There is a buyer for the Mansion," I blurted out when we reached the monument.

"You are kidding!"

"No, and it gets worse. It's Trevor Mitchell's father."

"This is awful. I thought our plan was working."

"I did, too. He plans to tear down the house and build a strip mall."

"Tear it down?" Alexander's warm brown eyes turned fiery red.

"I know. It's horrible. We did such a great job of convincing people that the Mansion was a money pit that no one wanted to buy it. Now they just want to tear it down. I messed everything up, Alexander. I ruined everything."

I sat down on a cemetery bench and covered my face with my hands.

"This isn't your fault, Raven," Alexander said, comforting me. His dark mood brightened. "He hasn't bought the house yet. There is still time."

"If we tell your parents, maybe they won't sell?"

"My father is set on selling. I've even faced him with that possibility. He says the new owner is entitled to do with the house as they wish. But how did you find this out? My father hasn't said anyone has expressed interest."

"I heard it straight from the horse's mouth: Trevor."

"There has to be something we can do. I don't want to move, and the Mansion is not worthless."

I turned toward his grandmother's monument and wished for an answer.

"We have to stop him. His father can't buy it. No one can. That house is your home. Our home. And most especially—your grandmother's." I got up and walked over to the monument. "Your grandmother Sterling built that house with love. For her—and her family."

"I know," he said. "It breaks my heart for so many reasons."

Alexander joined me at the monument. "It is my grandmother's house . . . and always will be."

"You're the only one who's taking care of it. I know your grandmother would be devastated if it were sold—or destroyed. There is no other buyer that that house means more to than you and her."

Then he turned to me. "You say the smartest things!"

"What do you mean?"

"I can't believe I didn't think of it sooner." Alexander was exuberant. He gave me a huge kiss and swung me around.

"What's going on?"

"The Mansion is for sale," he said with a grin. "And I know someone who is just dying to buy it."

I had no idea who Alexander had in mind to buy the Mansion. Whoever it was had to be rich and someone Alexander didn't mind hanging out in his grandmother's house. And how would that help him stay in Dullsville? My boyfriend promised me he'd let me in on his plan as soon as we met again.

The following sunset I met him at the boxcar.

"I couldn't sleep at all," I said impatiently as I snuck inside.

He took my hand and held me close.

"So tell me—who can you find to buy the Mansion?" I asked with a bit of hope in my voice.

"I turn eighteen in a few months," Alexander began. "And when I do, I'll be entitled to my inheritance. My grandmother was a very generous woman. So I figured it out—I'll be able to pay for the Mansion's upkeep."

I was wide-eyed.

"*I'll* buy the Mansion," he said proudly.

"That's a great idea!" I took his hands and danced around. "You are a genius."

"I don't have to move back to Romania if I have a place of my own here, right? And I think my grandmother would be happy that I used her money to keep the Mansion."

"I love that plan!" I squeezed my boyfriend and kissed him repeatedly. I was so proud of Alexander for his intellect. I was dating someone wise beyond his years.

"I'm almost legally an adult," he continued. "Then I'll be able to make my own decisions."

Alexander's maturity was like an aphrodisiac.

"You are hot—and brilliant!" I said, gushing.

"Don't get too excited. There is one hitch."

"Really? But I thought you said—"

"I'll need to put a deposit down and eventually pay closing costs. I do have money in the bank, but it isn't enough. I just need to come up with money for a down payment."

The only monthly fees I knew about were those charged at Dullsville's video store. I was clueless when it came to housing costs.

"But where are we going to come up with that kind of money?" I asked.

"Therein lays the problem."

"I only have a few hundred in the bank and about sixty in my drawer at home," I offered. "I'll ask my parents for a loan."

"Enough for a down payment on a house? They'll just give that to a sixteen-year-old girl?"

"No—to you," I said.

"Her seventeen-year-old boyfriend? I appreciate the thought, but I don't think that would go over well."

"How much money do we need?"

Alexander mouthed a number that was way higher than I had anticipated.

"Where can we find that kind of money?" I asked, stupefied.

"That part I haven't figured out yet. But we need to before Trevor's father cuts a check."

27

Naper Paper

I was under two deadlines: I had to raise enough money for Alexander before Trevor's father made an offer on the Mansion, and I needed to complete my essay—or start it—before our big presentation.

I had a hard time focusing on either. I didn't know how to raise money, and if we didn't figure out something quick, Alexander would be moving to Romania. To quell my nerves, I sat at my computer and tried to begin the essay.

But how did Mrs. Naper expect me to focus on a career or future when Alexander was going to be across the world? My only hope now was to enroll in the University of Transylvania. Even if I had good enough grades, was accepted, and could afford it, that would be at least two years away. By that time Alexander could be married—to someone else.

However, if I had a career now and not in five years, I'd be able to help Alexander with his house money. I tapped my fingers on my desk in frustration and tried to focus on the essay.

I'd really never thought much about what I'd want to do with my life other than becoming a vampire. How was I supposed to explain that to my classmates? I began thinking about what I loved—vampires, morbid music, hanging out in cemeteries. But what career would allow me to be me? A doctor? I couldn't imagine anyone feeling comfortable with me in a black surgical mask and dark scrubs coming at them with a scalpel. My patients would insist on healing themselves. A lawyer? I don't think the judge would permit miniskirts and monster boots in a courtroom. A teacher? The parents would pull their students out of my class.

And, did I want to spend the rest of my life in Dullsville—especially given the possibility that Alexander might not be here, too? I'd always been dying to get out of town, but when I met my true love all that changed. I once dreamed of a place where I wasn't an outsider anymore. And if Alexander returned to Romania, I'd be lonelier than I had been before.

Was I afraid of being true to myself in front of my English class? Was I too timid to explore everything I might really be able to become? Was I too nervous to share my dream of becoming a vampire or anything else I might choose? I'd always thought my character was just as important—if not more so—than the career I'd pursue. I had to be honest about that—especially now that I'd made fun of Trevor for not reporting his true desires. But did I really have the courage that I was telling him he lacked?

I took a breath and began writing. Words filled my head faster than I could type them. I wrote about my passions, no matter how ridiculous they might seem to Mrs. Naper and my classmates. The once-blank page was quickly being turned into an essay. I was in the zone and nothing was going to distract me.

When I finished my first draft, I made some notes for my presentation.

Careers are about making money, I thought, but a great career was doing what someone loved—and being paid for it. Trevor should be a professional soccer player. Billy Boy would be a scientist or computer programmer. And Alexander would be an artist. But wasn't he one already? He had already won first place in Hipsterville's Art Fair. Now he just needed to be paid for his artwork so he could buy the Mansion.

And then it hit me. Why hadn't I thought of it sooner?

We could sell Alexander's paintings in Dullsville's Annual Art Auction.

The Naper Paper proved to be more insightful than I'd ever imagined.

Convincing Alexander about my brilliant plan was another thing.

"The Dullsville auction," I said when we met inside the rail yard boxcar. "We'll sell your paintings in the auction."

"Are you kidding me? No one would buy my artwork."

Alexander stared at his paintings on the wall. "You heard my father. I paint more as a hobby. Raven, that auction is for professional artists."

"Alexander, these paintings are gorgeous. I don't need to be an expert to tell that these are valuable."

"You are just biased because you are my girlfriend."

"You won first prize in Hipsterville's Art Fair. Those voters weren't dating you. You are megatalented. If I've learned anything from my English assignment, it's that hobbies can turn into careers. And we are going to prove it."

"I don't think so—there must be some other way."

"There isn't time," I pleaded. "The auction is this week. It's the only way."

"I'm not prepared for the town to see my work—much less ask anyone to buy it," he said.

"You won't. I will."

"I don't know how to participate in an auction. Or even who to ask."

"Unfortunately or fortunately," I said, "I have a major connection to Dullsville's auction in the form of my perfectly evil English partner."

"I need to speak with you," I said to Trevor as soon as I saw him the following morning. He was getting out of his Camaro and sauntering toward school.

"Really?" he leered. "It will cost you. How about that kiss you didn't have time for before?"

"How do I put things in the art auction?" I asked, ignoring his come-on.

"What do you have of value?"

"I don't, but someone else does."

"So why doesn't that someone ask me?"

"Because I am acting as an agent."

"If you get ten percent, what do I get?" He shot me a sexy grin.

"How about what you *won't* get—a step on your foot or a kick to the shin?"

"You say the cutest things, Monster Girl. Sorry, I can't help you."

I tugged on his backpack. "I'm asking you as your English partner—be a humanitarian. I can still skip class on our assignment date and watch you fail from outside the window."

He weighed his options heavily. Then he reluctantly agreed.

"My mom is in charge of the auction. I suppose I can drive you there after school."

"I'll take my bike and meet you there."

"You think you can get into the country club looking like that? You'll need me to escort you."

Trevor had a point. I'd only frequented the upscale club when I was accompanied by my sports-obsessed father and forced to wear tennis whites. They didn't welcome the pins and studs that I was sporting now. "I'll meet you in the parking lot," I agreed.

He was surprised at my positive response and left for class with an extra spring in his step.

After school, I found Trevor sitting on the hood of his

Camaro—the whole soccer team was waiting around him as if he'd just won the World Cup.

Trevor opened the door to the Camaro. "Step inside."

His jock mates yelled, "Whoo hoo!"

I wasn't worried about my safety, but I was worried about my reputation. I didn't run with the in crowd—and at this point, I wanted to keep it that way.

Besides, I had something better than mace if Trevor decided to become friendly.

"Becky and Matt are coming, too," I said, as Dullsville's cutest couple caught up to me.

I felt victorious, but Trevor was unfettered.

"Of course," he said coyly. "We'll double."

I thought the alarm bells would sound when I entered the club and I'd be arrested by the fashion police. Though Becky and Matt were close behind, a staff member approached me.

"Can I help you?" a tall man in a green country club suit asked.

"I'm here with Trevor. Trevor Mitchell. He's parking the car."

"You are?" he asked, checking me out.

"There is a dress code, I know. But we are just passing through."

Just then my savior in khakis came through the door.

"Hi, Dave," Trevor said. "I'm here to see my mom."

"Hi, Trevor. How are you? Your mother's in the banquet hall." It was the first time in my life I was happy to be by Trevor's side.

We made our way down the orange-and-brown-patterned carpeted corridor. Unoriginal, hotel-inspired art lined the green painted walls.

Mrs. Mitchell was opening a cardboard box when she noticed Trevor walk in. She beamed as she stood up, then frowned when she saw me enter the room behind her son.

"Are you in trouble?" It was her first reaction.

"Raven wants to place something in the auction."

"Hello, Matt, Becky . . . Raven."

"Hello, Mrs. Mitchell," we responded. Mrs. Mitchell was like the teacher students dreaded having—chummy with those who excelled and short with those who didn't.

"That's very nice of you to help out your . . ." She hesitated, then glared at me. ". . . friends."

She, like Trevor, was skeptical that I was capable of participating in a high-society Dullsville auction. She tried hard to hide her contempt for me. But it was clear she didn't think I had anything of value to sell.

"This isn't for a school project, is it?" she asked. "This is an adult auction for collectors. We aren't auctioning off papier-mâché penguins made in art class."

"No," I said in my politest voice. Normally, I would say something snotty, but Alexander and the Mansion's fate were on the line. So I kissed up to her like she had never been kissed up to before.

"We are studying careers in English class and I thought what better way to see a successful woman than to watch her up close? Not only will I see how you organize this event, but I'll be able to see how an auction really works."

"Well . . . I had no idea," Mrs. Mitchell said, suddenly bright and charming. "What would you like to auction?"

"Paintings."

"From your father's collection? Is it an artist we know?"

I was afraid to tell her they were from a teen vampire.

"No. A young European talent."

"European?" Mrs. Mitchell asked, her eyes almost popping out of her head. "It would be nice to showcase someone on the rise. Of course, I'd need to see it first."

"Someone will bring it by," I chimed in.

"Good. Then fill out this form. And bring the artwork to me by the middle of the week—no later than five o'clock."

"That's it?" Trevor asked on my behalf.

"That's it. I'll set aside an area just for you."

"Thanks," I said.

"Why don't you stay and I can show you the real behind-the-scenes goings-on in event planning. It might help you with your report. Then I can run you home afterward."

"That's okay, Mom," Trevor interjected before I could. "I have to take her back before soccer practice tonight."

"Well then. Remember, all pieces need to be checked in before five."

Alexander wouldn't be able to drop the paintings off before sunset. And how was I going to lug all his artwork there on my bike? We'd have to find someone strong and not bound by the curfew of daylight.

I just hoped Jameson had developed some muscles from vacuuming.

"I'll drop you two off first. Then I'll take Raven home," Trevor told us when we raced out of the club parking lot. At this point I wished I had stayed with his mother and rode home with her.

"Oh, that's okay. I'm going to Raven's house," Becky said.

Trevor's expression turned from triumph to torment. He dropped Matt off in silence and didn't speak the rest of the way. He barely let us out before he sped away.

"I owe you big-time, Becky," I said when we were safely on the sidewalk.

Unlike Becky, I didn't have my own truck. "Want to ride on the handlebars or the seat?"

"How about I wait for Matt to come back and pick me up?" she suggested. "Then you can avoid leg cramps."

We sat down on the front steps. "I can tell you whose paintings are going to be put up on the auction block," I began.

Becky's face sparkled. "Whose?"

"It's a total colossal secret."

"Are there any other kind?"

"Not even Matt can know."

She paused. "Forever?"

"No, just until the auction is over."

"I can totally do that."

She leaned in close.

And I said in my softest voice, "The paintings I'm auctioning off are Alexander's."

"That's awesome!" she declared. "But why is it a secret?"

"Because we don't want anyone to know he's the artist. We're afraid that no one will buy them if they know they're from a teenager. And one that lives in the Mansion."

"I see your point. But what will you do with the money?"

"This is an even bigger secret. We plan to buy the Mansion."

It wasn't long before Matt pulled into the driveway.

"What's up?"

"Nothing," Becky said as she got into his car. "Nothing is up. And I don't have any more to say about it, either. And for that matter, I never will."

A confused Matt drove off as Becky looked out the window and smiled.

28

Head of the Class

The following morning we sat through several painfully boring English presentations. Students had revelations of being Web designers, pharmacists, and restaurateurs. I prayed we wouldn't get to Trevor and me, but the clock had ten minutes remaining. My prayers weren't answered.

"So what did you learn about yourselves?" Mrs. Naper asked.

Trevor, always the star, had no inhibitions about being the center of attention. He sprang up next to Mrs. Naper's desk while I walked past my classmates as if I were headed for the guillotine.

"When I was in kindergarten," Trevor began, "like most boys, I wanted to be a superhero." A few girls in the front row giggled. Trevor stopped and shot them a cold stare until the girls glanced away. "Of course, I'm not that kid anymore," he continued, "but I do like action, speed, and competition. What I've learned from this assignment and the interview is that when you are a kid, you don't worry about what others think of your ideas. And your dreams have no boundaries. It might be easy, predictable, and even safe to follow in my parents' professions. But my essay is about how a superhero has courage, and it takes courage to follow your dream. And my goal . . . ," he began, and then turned to me, "is to be a professional soccer player."

"Tell us something we don't know," a Pradabee said, flipping through her notebook.

I was really surprised at Trevor's speech. I had challenged my nemesis with my earlier assessment of him and he felt he had to prove to me that he wasn't the coward I thought he was. I wondered if I hadn't said anything, if Trevor would have stood here proclaiming he wanted to be a real estate developer like his dad.

The class applauded and Mrs. Naper grinned at her student pet. "Very interesting and well spoken, Trevor," she complimented. "Now we have just enough time for Raven's presentation before the bell rings."

I gazed out at my fellow students. They glared back like I was the lead act at a freak show.

"When I was young," I began, "I wanted to be a vampire."

My classmates snickered. I pursed my lips and clutched my fist.

"Settle down," Mrs. Naper commanded.

I looked to Becky, who gave me the thumbs-up sign.

"And since then," I continued, "I've lived my life in a way and style that reflects that. It never mattered to me what other people wore—"

"Obviously," I heard someone say.

"Or *said*," I continued. "And because of this I've always been an outcast. Just by being me. So I imagine that I'll find a profession that suits me—perhaps being an editor of my own goth fashion mag," I said enthusiastically. "But as we are looking toward our future, I'm not sure it matters *what* we want to be but rather *who* we want to be. Someone honest or deceitful? Someone kind or cruel? Someone loyal or unfaithful? In any profession we can elect to be any of those things. I think this assignment is not only about what we choose to *do* but about who we choose to *be*. I choose to always be loyal to myself."

I stood in front of my classmates, waiting for their response. No laughter. No snickering. No booing. I turned to Mrs. Naper and Trevor, who both appeared stunned.

Just then the bell rang.

Relieved the assignment was finally over, I followed Trevor and handed in my essay. As the students filed out of class, I overheard a cheerleader speaking with her friend.

"I know I said I want to be a model, but what I meant was a *nice* model."

"Yeah," said one of the Pradabees. "When I have my designer clothing line, I'll give ten percent of the goods to charity."

After the two girls left, a member of the band was suddenly standing next to me. "I said I wanted to be a teacher, but I really haven't decided what I want to do," he shared with me. "You made me feel that it was okay to focus on myself for a while. And the rest will follow."

"I think it will," I said reassuringly.

Mrs. Naper put Trevor's and my essays in her folder. "In all the years I've been giving this assignment, yours and Trevor's presentations were two of the best." She gloated.

Trevor put his arm around me before I could bat it away. "Guess that means we'll be working together again very soon," he said triumphantly, and disappeared into the hallway.

Becky handed me my backpack. "Seems like your presentation was more powerful than you planned. Maybe you should be a motivational speaker."

"Can I wear combat boots?" I asked.

"You'll be the only one," she said, and dragged me out of class.

29

Auction

I'd never attended, nor had reason to attend, the gala affair known as Dullsville's Annual Art Auction. My parents were more than happy and quite surprised that I was trading in an evening at the cemetery for one spent at the country club. My dad actually gave me the keys to his SUV since Jameson would be driving the Sterlings later. I chauffeured the unknown and mysterious artist, Alexander Sterling, to the event.

The country club's parking lot was as huge as a theme park's and seemed miles away from the club. Lexuses, Bentleys, and BMWs lined the front entrance. Anyone who was anyone valeted their car and saved all exercise for their chats at the bar.

I pulled into a slot a football field away and joked to Alexander that we should wait for the shuttle bus.

"You should actually be arriving in a limo," I said to

my very handsome and quite nervous boyfriend.

All the members were dressed to the nines. Hats, scarves, and enormously overpriced sequined clutch purses dotted the affair. Art collectors from around the area hobnobbed with the members.

All the bigwigs in town were present, including the mayor, Mr. and Mrs. Mitchell, and Mr. Berkley. The snooty members were buzzing around, acting like they owned the multiacre building. Anyone who was anyone was at the auction. It was rumored that paintings, sculptures, and jewelry would be sold. Since not much else goes on in town, and since it attracted out-of-towners, too, this was a major event.

Annual Art Auction signs led the way to the banquet room I'd been to previously with Trevor. It was there that a ticket table had been set up. We waited in line behind several women decked out in their Sunday best. When it was our turn to buy tickets, the seller was surprised by her oddly attired customers. But I wasn't bothered. I acted like I didn't even notice, just like Mrs. Sterling did. Alexander was prepared to pay, but I insisted. "You need to save all the money you can," I said.

There was a buzz of self-importance. Old and young wealth rubbing elbows with other thoroughbred moneymakers. Sotheby's it wasn't, but the auction was a close second.

Members gawked at Alexander and me with disapproval. I couldn't wait until Mrs. Sterling arrived with her umbrella and turned heads.

The bar was filled with gossip, smoke, and drinkers. I

was dying to get a soda, but I wasn't sure what the etiquette was. Would I have to pay for it? Tip? I opted to wait until my parents showed up.

Cookies and cakes were spread out on a few banquet tables and I managed to gulp down a few, but Alexander passed.

Alexander was as nervous as I was when I attended his parents' first dinner party. My boyfriend was used to being sequestered in a mansion, with Jameson and me as his only companions. Now he was in the midst of Dullsville's finest. Not only were there a lot of people, but his paintings were going to be sold in front of the entire town.

Outside the banquet hall, a table was set up for a silent auction fund-raiser, with such goodies as spa treatments, restaurant gift certificates, and discounts at Armstrong Travel.

As we approached the auction room, I grew anxious, too. This event could send Alexander packing his bags to Romania and me to my bedroom, grieving for the next ten years.

The auction room seemed like the ones I'd seen in movies. Lines of folding chairs were placed like pews in a church, facing a podium and an easel. We tried to slip in unnoticed, but for us that was impossible. Alexander and I grabbed two seats in the back, behind two tall club members.

I was ready to kick anyone who scoffed at my boyfriend's artwork.

This was a huge night for Alexander. He wasn't used to being around so many people. He fidgeted in his chair and I clasped his hand reassuringly.

"If you are really uncomfortable, we can leave," I offered. "We don't have to stay."

"No. I'm not leaving," Alexander said. "And neither are you. We are staying to see this thing through."

Dullsville's elite began entering the room in full fanfare. Alexander was the only true royal one, but the club members entered as if they were expecting their names to be announced like kings and queens.

Jameson entered on the arm of Ruby White, his girlfriend, along with Janice Armstrong, her business partner and my former employer at Armstrong Travel Agency.

Mr. Mitchell, an older version of Trevor complete with moussed blond hair and khakis, arrived in the company of other millionaires and sat in the front row. Mr. Berkley came in a few minutes later and sat a few rows behind him.

With every person's entrance, my heart beat faster and my hands grew hotter.

My parents finally arrived and spent a fair amount of time greeting everyone they knew.

My mom eventually spotted us, and she and my dad came over.

"I think it's wonderful that you two came to the auction," my dad said, shaking Alexander's hand.

"Maybe next year you can auction off your paintings, Alexander," my mom said.

"Sarah, we'd better get seats before it fills up," my dad suggested. "Good luck," they said, and found two empty chairs in the middle.

I felt a sudden commotion as members were focused

on something out in the hallway.

Just then Mr. and Mrs. Sterling entered the room. Her open black and red umbrella was in hand, and she wore a skin-tight camisole dress and monster-size heels. Mr. Sterling walked in with his skull cane, wearing a suit, a flashy green tie, and his cape.

A huge smile spread across my face.

A few women fanned themselves with their auction signs. No one talked to the Sterlings, but everyone talked about them. Whispers ensued as the gossipmongers were in top form.

The members were very curious about the locals—who arrived with who and what they were wearing—and just as curious about the strangers' conservative fashion choices. The Sterlings upstaged everyone in their attire.

The only ones who greeted them were my parents and Mr. Berkley.

I held up my hand to wave them over, but Alexander quickly clutched it.

"I want us to be alone on this."

Mr. and Mrs. Sterling eventually sat next to Jameson and crew.

Finally, Mrs. Mitchell stepped up to the podium. "Welcome to our annual auction. In a moment, I'll bring out your auctioneer. We'll be presenting art in many of its forms—pottery, paintings, sculptures, and wood designs. Thank you all for coming tonight. Good luck and good bidding."

The auctioneer, an elderly gentleman dressed in a suit, came out to the podium. A volunteer placed a glass-blown vase bejeweled with sparkling gems on a table. Its image was enlarged on a video screen behind the podium.

I was on the edge of my folding chair.

Mrs. Mitchell read a brief description of the vase. "The bidding starts at five hundred dollars."

"Five hundred dollars. That's a lot of moola!" I whispered.

"Shh."

"Whatever you do, don't raise your hand," I said, teasing. "No matter how much you want to buy it for me."

Alexander wasn't laughing. "I didn't price my work very high. Maybe I should have."

"Your paintings are much more valuable than a dumb vase."

Signs began to wave and the bidding price immediately soared. Within minutes the vase sold for over a thousand dollars.

"I wish I had something fancy to sell," I said, seeing dollar signs before my eyes. "I could make millions."

Even though I wasn't bidding, I got caught up in the frenzy. I could see why Dullsvillians waited all year for this event. It was like high-priced bingo, everyone waiting on the edge of their seats, wanting the glamorous prize, or hoping their item might make them millions—more than they already had, anyway.

A covered painting was brought to the easel. They unveiled it to a few gasps and whispers. It was a landscape of the country club itself. By Alexander. I was so proud, his artwork was displayed for all to see. No one even knew

Alexander had painted it.

"This is a painting from a rising European artist," Mrs. Mitchell said. "There was little information about the artist, but as you can see, the work speaks for itself. A one-of-a-kind original painting. The artist states, 'The inspiration was the beauty that unfolds when I open my eyes in this town.'"

The audience whispered and sat up as if they were eyeing a museum piece.

"Bidding starts at five hundred," the auctioneer began.

"Five hundred?" I heard someone say in front of us.

"I can't believe we're doing this. This whole thing is going to blow up in my face. I can kiss the Mansion and you good-bye," Alexander said in my ear.

"Five hundred is a steal," the person in front of me continued. "I bid seven hundred."

I turned to Alexander in amazement.

"Eight hundred," another said, holding up their sign.

"Nine hundred," still another shouted.

"Do I hear nine-fifty?" the auctioneer asked.

"A thousand," the first bidder answered.

"Eleven hundred? Do I hear eleven hundred?"

The second bidder held up her sign.

"Fifteen hundred—"

The signs went up until it reached two thousand dollars.

"Sold for two thousand," the auctioneer proclaimed, and slammed his gavel.

I grabbed my boyfriend and hugged him with all my

might. Even though I knew Alexander's art was priceless, I was so proud his pictures commanded so much money. The most money I'd ever made in sales was three dollars from my chocolate milk stand in the middle of summer. And my dad paid for it.

The members couldn't contain their comments and began to buzz about the painting.

The highest bidder was the president of the country club. "I'd like to hang it here in the club for all to see," he said proudly.

I was not only flabbergasted because Alexander's artwork sold for so much money but because my ghostly gothic vampire boyfriend's work was going to hang in Dullsville's conservative country club.

A piece of jewelry was shown next. Now I was fidgeting in my chair, anticipating another Sterling painting going on the auction block.

After a six-foot-high sculpture of a mother and child was sold, a narrative quilt was auctioned off.

Then another covered painting was placed on the easel. When it was uncovered, it was revealed to be Dullsville's Main Street.

"Another beautiful piece. It captures the charm that is our town," Mrs. Mitchell said.

The painting was of the shops on the square. Shirley's bakery. The fountain. Children eating ice cream. Looking at it made me feel I was standing on the square with the townspeople.

"Lovely," the couple in front of us commented.

"Starting price one thousand dollars."

Several signs immediately rose.

"Fifteen hundred," the auctioneer called.

Several signs kept flying up at the same time.

The bidding war increased and finally ended with a winning bid of four thousand dollars.

I squeezed Alexander's hand so hard I thought it was going to break off.

I made a quick note of how much Alexander had made.

When the next item was a mosaic mural, the crowd sighed.

They perked up when the following item was a covered painting. When it was unveiled to be a painting of the town from the "European artist," everyone was on the edge of their seats; the blue bloods were anticipating a sign war.

This time it was the front of Hatsy's Diner. I could almost hear the fifties music playing and smell the aroma of french fries cooking.

"Starting price one thousand five hundred dollars."

"I'll bid two thousand," Mr. Berkley said.

"Two thousand five hundred," another shouted.

"Three thousand," still another shouted.

"Do I hear three thousand five hundred?"

Mr. Berkley held his sign high.

"Do I hear four thousand?"

Another bidder raised his sign.

"Do I hear four thousand five hundred?"

Mr. Berkley raised his sign.

"Five thousand," Ruby White suddenly burst out.

"Going once, twice . . . Sold for five thousand dollars."

I cheered, but when the couple in front of me turned around, I tried to play it cool.

When another painting was put on the easel, the members became very excited again. They thirsted to get their hands on an original painting by this hot new artist.

When they revealed it, it was a portrait of flowers, obviously painted by an artist other than Alexander. Mrs. Mitchell went on to talk about this artist, but the bidding didn't start high, nor did it skyrocket.

The crowd waited impatiently for the next painting to be presented.

And when it was again one of the European artist's creations, the hands began waving.

It was now becoming clear to me after seeing these paintings one by one—the cemetery under the soft glow of moonlight; the rail yard, with its bright-colored boxcars and sunfire yellow weeds; the front of the high school, its American flag blowing in the wind; the swings underneath a blue sky at Evans Park; the drive-in running an old movie—that even though Alexander only visited these places at night, he was seeing Dullsville in brilliant colors and happy hues rather than the dark and dismal black and white I'd seen it in my whole life. These were the places we'd visited together. My heart melted seeing that I'd had something to do with Alexander's happiness here, and that his vivid impressions were of our experiences together.

Finally they revealed the last painting. But this painting

was unlike the others. It was a picture of me.

The members sighed.

"That's not the European artist," many of them said.

"No, that's not his work."

"Bidding starts at one thousand dollars."

No one raised their sign.

I quickly calculated my notes and realized we had fallen short of what Alexander needed.

My dad looked around. Here was a picture of his daughter and no one was buying it.

"Do I hear one thousand?"

"I'll bid one thousand," my dad said, waving his sign proudly.

Then Jameson got into the game. "One thousand five hundred," he called.

"Two thousand," my dad said.

"Do I hear two thousand five hundred?" the auctioneer asked. I peered around. No signs were waved. "Going once, going twice."

My heart dropped. We'd raised a lot of money, but we hadn't raised enough to buy the mansion.

"We're short," I said to Alexander. "Do I hear two thousand five hundred?" I shouted.

Alexander grabbed my arm.

"We have to get the bidding up," I whispered to him.

"Two thousand five hundred." Jameson raised his sign.

"Two thousand five hundred. Going once, going twice."

"Three thousand dollars," a new voice, coming from the back of the room, called.

"Do I hear three thousand five hundred?" the auctioneer asked. He banged his gavel. "Then sold for three thousand."

Alexander and I stood up and hugged each other. We were so ecstatic we didn't care that anyone saw us. And I was too excited to wonder who the mystery bidder was.

"Now we just have to get that money to Mr. Berkley before Mr. Mitchell does."

A few volunteers brought out all the auctioned items and displayed them so that everyone could take a last look at what they'd won and what they'd lost.

Mr. Sterling put on his reading glasses and examined the tiny inscription about the rising artist whose work had quickly sold out.

Then he turned straight back to us.

The club members were milling about, talking to one another and discussing the auction. But there was only one member I wanted to speak to: Mr. Berkley. I weaved between the members until I spotted him.

After a brief conversation with him, I raced over to Alexander, who was waiting by the kitchen.

"Here," I said, showing him Mr. Berkley's card. "You have an appointment tomorrow night at eight."

We lingered for a few minutes while the crowd talked excitedly about the evening.

"I hear the artist is here," I overheard a patron say.

"He is?" another asked. "I'd love to meet him."

"The artist has been here the whole time," one woman said.

"Which one is he?" a man asked.

"The one in the cowboy hat?" another man inquired.

"No, he must have been the one with long gray hair," the woman said.

"I think you should meet your public," I said.

"I'm not sure that now is the time," he said anxiously, his face white as a ghost.

Alexander had done enough tonight. Though he was beaming from his sudden acceptance, he was too humble to accept fame.

We ducked through the kitchen and out a side exit to the opposite end of the club where the members were exiting. We were afraid that if anyone found out the artist was Alexander, they'd demand their money back. We were leaving through the patio exit when we were blocked by a thin wooden stick.

We froze.

Mr. Sterling stepped in front of us.

Alexander and I didn't know what to do.

"You have your grandmother's gift," he said in his thick Romanian accent.

"It's just a hobby," Alexander said.

"I think you've just proved to me—and to yourself—that it's more than that. I've found that new artist I was looking for. I just didn't realize he'd been here the whole time."

Mrs. Naper handed back our graded English career essays. Matt and Trevor and all the other jocks were off preparing for a pep rally, so I wasn't going to have to face Trevor. Unfortunately, that was the only thing that made school exciting.

"I'm hoping you can give the papers to your partners," Mrs. Naper said to us.

"I sure will," Becky said, excited. "We got an A."

"No surprise," I said.

"What did you get?" Becky asked.

I opened Trevor's Dullsville High School folder and saw the scarlet A next to his name. "Well, Trevor got an A, of course." I designed my folder like it was the cover of a gothic magazine, complete with pasted headlines, gothic fashions, and teasers. I opened it and hoped for a good letter in the alphabet. "So did I!"

After school, I biked over to Oakley Woods.

Mrs. Mitchell answered the door. "Hello, Raven."

"Hi, Mrs. Mitchell. Is—"

"It was quite a surprise to learn that the European artist was actually Alexander."

I waited. Maybe we had embarrassed her at the auction.
It was as if at any moment the Wicked Witch of the West
would point her broom at me.

"I must say your boyfriend is truly talented. What a
wonderful surprise to know that we had such a fine artist
among us. It's a shame he'll be moving. We'd love to have
his work in the auction next year."

"Uh . . . thanks, Mrs. Mitchell," I said, relieved. "Is
Trevor home? We got our grades back from our English
assignment."

"Come on in. Trevor's upstairs."

I quickly raced up the main staircase and found
Trevor's bedroom door ajar.

I tapped it. "Hello. Soccer Boy?"

No answer.

I could have waited in the hallway, but that wouldn't
have been any fun at all.

Trevor's room was still a shrine to himself. I nosed
around his awards and trophies and framed soccer jerseys.

I noticed something large was covered in the corner.
Maybe it was a mirror.

I snuck over to it and pulled back the cloth so I could
take a peek.

Staring back at me was *me*—the final painting of

Alexander's sold at the auction. I was shocked.

I heard the door begin to creak open and quickly recovered the painting.

"What are you doing here?" Trevor asked.

"Uh . . . I wanted to tell you we got an A."

"So?"

"I just thought you'd like to know."

"What else would we have gotten? You're not used to getting good grades."

I had done my duty and there was nothing left to say. I started for the door when he blocked my escape.

I was alone with Trevor in his room—a dangerous place to be.

"Anything else you'd like to do?" he asked.

I wanted to say, *Get that picture back*, but I sensed Trevor wanted a stolen kiss—a treasure that was far more valuable than an A.

I'd never let myself succumb to that. Even if I wasn't dating Alexander, nothing would ever be sacred or special with Trevor.

I didn't mention seeing the painting. I was too touched and slightly bothered that he'd spent his money on a picture of me. It was ironic that Trevor would be the one to help Alexander buy back the Mansion and divert his father from his plans.

It would be awesome to throw it in his face. But I didn't dare do that to my partner.

I offered my hand instead. I figured I was safe with that.

He held it like he didn't want to let it go.

His golden hair was perfect against his suntanned face. I knew he wanted to kiss me—and I wasn't sure whether it was love or lust or just because I was a girl alone in his room.

"I know there's a part of you that wonders what it would be like," Trevor said.

"I already know," I said. "The cheerleaders have it written on the bathroom walls."

I withdrew my hand and left his room before he tried to hold any other part of me.

Hello, Miss Raven," Jameson said as I entered the Mansion. "Alexander will be down in a moment."

I waited in the parlor room.

"Hello, Raven," Mrs. Sterling said, stepping into the room. "Did you like the auction? I thought it was a blast."

"Yes, I'm so proud of Alexander."

"I always knew he was talented. But Constantine—he knows now," she said with a wink.

"I just got off the phone with Mr. Berkley," Mr. Sterling said in a low voice as he entered the parlor. "He said someone made an offer and they are going to come for a tour of the Mansion."

"When will they be here?" Mrs. Sterling asked. "We already have company," she said, referring to me.

"He told me he should be here by now."

"I hate lateness," Mrs. Sterling said. "It is so rude."

Alexander came into the parlor.

"A prospective buyer is coming to the house. We'll be able to sell the Mansion and return . . . Where is that man?" his father asked, agitated.

"He's here," Alexander said.

"Where, standing in the hallway?"

"No, standing right in front of you."

"I don't understand."

"I am going to buy the Mansion."

"You?"

Mr. and Mrs. Sterling were bewildered.

"I've been trying to tell you," Alexander said. "This is my home. In this house, in this town, with this girl." He smiled at me.

I was so proud of Alexander for taking charge of his life but was sure I was going to be in big trouble with his parents. I was ready for them to scream at me or throw me out.

"Maybe I should be leaving . . ." I said.

"No, stay. You need to hear this," Alexander said, and turned to his parents.

"Don't you see? I've been successful on my own since I arrived here. And these accomplishments are because I met the girl of my dreams, Raven."

His parents looked at me, and I felt an immense pressure build.

"Because of Jagger, I've had to leave Romania several times. And now that I've helped the Maxwells, I'm supposed to leave this town. I'm not leaving anymore."

"How did you plan to purchase the Mansion?" Mr. Sterling asked, still shocked.

"I'm going to use the money I raised from the auction as a down payment. And when I turn eighteen, I'm going to pay off the monthly mortgage with my trust fund."

"That money is for your future," his mother said. "Your grandmother wanted you to have it for that reason."

"This *is* my future, Mother. Grandmother wouldn't want it any other way. And neither would I. This mansion may not mean anything to you. But it means everything to me."

"I don't understand," his mom said. "I want you to live with us."

"I know, Mother," he said, and held her hands. "But I'm almost eighteen. I could be going off to college, taking night classes. Instead, I'll be here. Painting and being with Raven."

Mr. Sterling paced around the room, wiping his hair off his brow. "This is quite a shock, you must understand. I didn't realize, Alexander, how you have grown. That you are so much like your grandmother. That you both are. . . ."

Alexander and I felt a glimmer of hope.

"When I saw that you were the artist behind those paintings, it was clear to me then that you'd found a home here. But . . ." He paused. "There is no way you are buying the Mansion."

"I am!" Alexander said boldly.

"No, Son, I'm taking it off the market. It is rightfully yours. There is no reason you should have to pay for it."

"But, I want to—"

"I know. And that is the reason you shouldn't. Because you care so much about so many things. I'm not allowing you to buy the house from me. We'll invest the money you earned. My mother must be watching over us right now. I know she is smiling at you—and frowning at me. I made a big mistake looking at others when it was you I should have been showcasing. My own son. Jameson, get Mr. Berkley on the line."

"Mother, I'm sorry—"

She put her fingers to her lips. "You are the kind of man I always wanted you to become—you just became one a lot faster than I was ready for."

"I have to confess I haven't slept well since we decided to sell the house," Mr. Sterling added.

Jameson walked into the parlor.

"Jameson, there has been a change in plans. The Mansion will remain a Sterling legacy. Mrs. Sterling and I will be returning to Romania, but Alexander will live here. I understand you will be returning with us and we'll find another butler for Alexander."

Jameson stood as straight as he could and took a deep breath. "Sir, if you don't mind, I have a reason for staying in town, too," Jameson confessed. "Alexander is not the only one with a soul mate."

Jameson stood outside the Mansion, packing the Sterlings' remaining bags into the trunk of the Mercedes.

I held Alexander, who was anxious, around the waist. I wasn't able to calm him.

A gentle rain began to fall, and within a few minutes a trickle turned into a shower, but Alexander and I stayed put.

Mr. and Mrs. Sterling descended the front steps of the Mansion.

"It was lovely meeting you, Raven. We hope to see you again soon," Mrs. Sterling said, offering me her hand. "Welcome to the family."

Instead of taking her hand, I leaned in and hugged her hard. It was as if I were breaking the rules and hugging the queen of England, but I didn't care. This woman meant the world to me.

"Alexander, darling, you know I love you," she said with a strain in her lyrical voice. She was trying to mask her emotion. She kissed her son good-bye on both cheeks.

She stood back as Mr. Sterling extended his hand to mine. "It was a pleasure to have met you, Raven. We are all happier for it." He gave me polite kisses, one on each side of my face.

"We will not be such strangers anymore," he said to Alexander. "I'll await your next round of paintings."

Alexander's eyes lit up as he shook his father's hand.

"Thanks, Dad," he said.

Both men were surprised by his sudden affection.

"Well, we must be off," his father finally said. But there was something missing from Mrs. Sterling's wardrobe as we all stood in the downpour.

"Where is your parasol?" I asked.

"Who needs an umbrella in the rain?" she said, and stepped into the car.

We continued to stand there as the car slowly pulled away and drove down the Mansion's drive, past the gate, and into the street. Mrs. Sterling didn't look back. Perhaps if she did, she would never have been able to leave.

I felt sad, for Alexander and for me.

Tears welled in my eyes, and I couldn't help but frown.

"Why are you crying? I thought you'd be happy," Alexander said, wiping a tear from my face.

"I thought I'd be, too," I said. "I didn't want you to move, Alexander. But I didn't want them to either."

Alexander gave me a soft kiss in the rain. As the car disappeared, he put his arm around me and led me back inside my second home—the Sterling Mansion on Benson Hill.

Acknowledgments

I'd like to thank the following fabulous people for their expertise and guidance in my career—Katherine Tegen, Ellen Levine, and Julie Lansky.

And my wonderful family—Dad, Mom, Mark, and Ben, and in-laws Jerry, Hatsy, Hank, Wendy, Emily, and Max—for their support.